Katie Bloomstrom

The Trouble With St. John
A Samantha Stone Novel

For my sweet Rhino.
May I someday help you reach your goal of getting a really big tractor.

Now that this chapter of my blog diary is complete, I can hardly believe all the things that happened actually happened. I mean, the last thing I thought when I boarded the plane to St. John for my un-honeymoon was that I'd wind up right in the middle of a real live jewelry heist mystery complete with double crossers, sneaky photo takers, sexy island dwellers, attempted kidnappings, and at least one dead body. I don't know about anyone else, but I think that's kind of a lot of stuff to have happen in just one week.

But I'm getting way ahead of myself. In order to properly tell this story, I need to start at the beginning. The time I like to call…er – well, the beginning. I guess.

Whatever.

Introduction - Part I

My name is Samantha Stone. Unfortunately, everyone I know calls me Sammy. Not Sam. *Sammy.* Like I'm a nine-year-old in pigtails whose favorite fun pastime is coloring in her Monster High coloring book.

In reality, I'm twenty-eight. I hate being called *Sammy*, I don't have pigtails, and I don't like to color. Not anymore, at least. Okay, maybe I do still color sometimes. With my niece. Whatever.

I live in Minnesota, which is pretty much the worst state out of all the states. Plus, instead of living in one of the two partially-acceptable parts of Minnesota – the parts with enticing company headquarters and lofts and posh restaurants and hipsters and craft beers and things – I live in a long forgotten, half-dead place called Elkton, located about three hours southwest of anyplace worth mentioning at all. I've lived in Elkton all my life, along with 1,396 other sorry souls who have all lived in Elkton forever and will continue to live in Elkton until the day they die.

Nothing exciting has ever happened in Elkton, and I highly doubt anything ever will. Instead of enticing company headquarters, we have Peterson's Meat Packing – a stupid, smelly place that exports elk and elk-related products to other, better companies. Instead of lofts, we have houses from the 1970s that come complete with floral wallpaper, plastic couch covers, and red shag carpeting. Instead of posh restaurants, we have bars. Shitty, hole-in-the-wall bars. Fourteen of them, to be exact. This makes our bar-to-person ratio the best in the whole state! Oh, and instead of hipsters and craft beers, we have acid washed jeans, scrunchies, perms, bedazzled sweatshirts, and Johnnie Walker. Lots and lots of Johnnie Walker.

Elkton doesn't even have its own shopping mall. That's in the next town over. We do have a Super Walmart though. It has a little pretzel stand inside that sells a variety of pretzel flavors and dipping sauces and is, unfortunately, where most of Elkton hangs out on the weekends. Those too young to go to the bars, anyway.

Aside from the Super Walmart and all the bars and the meat plant, Elkton also boasts a Fleet Farm, a gas station, a seedy pawn shop, two liquor stores, three churches, four elk farms, and one library. Oh, we also have a very questionable adult video store/gun shop.

Our dentist/physician, Dr. Brad, works out of his basement, as does Vera, our resident hair stylist. The police chief, whose name is Chomps Douglas, doubles as the fireman who doubles as the town's plumber/electrician who doubles as the Pastor down at the Evangelical Free. But they're all the same guy. They're all Chomps. When Chomps gets sick, the whole town goes on a rampage, drinking Johnnie Walker and breaking laws and questioning their faith and setting things on fire.

Since Elkton is so boring and worthless, most Elktonites become alcoholics by the age of 14. Then they drop out of school and get jobs at the meat factory or the Fleet Farm. They proceed to get perms, start wearing scrunchies, and eventually spend their weekends scrapbooking, drinking, and bedazzling their sweatshirts. Once they make their first hot dish, their lives are officially over.

I used to be one of those people – the alcoholic bedazzlers – but then I met Colin.

Colin is my fiancé. He's an artist from the big city – Minneapolis, I mean. We met last year at one of Colin's fancy art gallery things and, in a few short days, we're getting married! Then my real life will finally start. My life away from Elkton and all its loser dumbness anyway.

Colin is so wonderful and loves me so much that he got me an iPad for my wedding gift to prove it. It's the only iPad in all of Elkton! And it came complete with its own wireless keyboard thingie in a special wireless keyboard case! When my mom saw it for the first time, she asked me if it was one of those Gameboys she'd heard about from Tammy Pedersen, her backyard neighbor. Try explaining an iPad to a woman who thinks the cordless telephone is the height of technological sophistication. And who literally just heard about Gameboys even though the first one came out in like 1989. (Hint: You can't explain anything to a person like that.)

Of course, I don't really know what to do with the iPad and its accompanying wireless keyboard, but I want Colin to think that I love it and use it adequately for lots of interesting things –

aside from just playing Solitaire and reading *Perez Hilton* all the time. So I've decided to start one of those computer diaries. You know, a blog sort of thing. Like Bridget Jones, but with a fancy wireless keyboard instead of a notebook and a sad Minnesotan accent instead of a posh foreign one.

Hey – it's better than coloring in my Monster High coloring book, right? Not that I have one or anything.

Okay, I'm off to the Super Walmart with Amanda (my very best girlfriend) to check out the what's happening, grab a cinnamon sugar pretzie, and select my eye shadow colors for the "Big Day." Hurrah!

What an exciting life I live.

Introduction – Part II

Things to do on un-honeymoon:
1. Forget about Colin and all Colin-related things.
2. Work on tan and transform from pale freckled Midwesterner to glowy amazing travel goddess.
3. Splash about in the ocean as salt water good for the hair and skin.
4. Drink beachy cocktails and flirt with glowy island men.
5. Catch up on sleep and pretend there is a sexy man in bed with me, even though there is not and likely never will be ever again.
6. Change personality and develop positive, sunny outlook.
7. Read massive historical travel novel; become well-read person with interesting comments and perspectives.
8. Obtain new job and life.

Things not to do on un-honeymoon:
1. Wallow, cry, whack attack, or feel bad about self.
2. Think about Colin or any Colin-related things.
3. Sob uncontrollably in front of others.
4. Blame self for wedding-day dumpage.
5. Mix alcohol and prescription medications.
6. Mix alcohol and sexual encounters with glowy island men.
7. Call Colin repeatedly and leave sobby drunken messages, even though I've already done that like a hundred times. At least.

8. Think bad thoughts about self, especially state of hair and skin.

9. Think bad thoughts about any of the following: Colin, awful job, demon boss, dumb friends who bail on un-honeymoon last minute, Colin, boss.

Part One
The Epical Fail That Led Me to This Horrendous Place in My Life, and Other Things

Date: Sunday
Time: Noonish
Location: Smelly half-seat on minuscule airplane, en route to tropical, hopefully sunny island of St. John.
Day Rating (So Far): Zero stars.

How do I even begin to describe this horrible, dreadful start to my honeymoon. *Un*-honeymoon, I mean. Obviously.

I suppose we could start here:
Stupid small-town girl falls in love with a wonderful floppy haired artist only to find out, on wedding day, that he's a lying, relationship-bailing asshole who disappeared into thin air and turned off his cell phone.

Or here:
Stupid small-town girl is forced to stand up at her own wedding and inform her own guests that her untrustworthy artist fiancé has disappeared into thin air and turned off his cell phone; elderly, crinkle-skinned grandparents who risked stroke and premature death to travel cross-country for the un-wedding become mean and overly critical; un-friends seem secretly happy for loser girl and promise to turn un-honeymoon into girls' getaway only to bail last minute.

Or maybe here:
Stupid small-town girl is forced to stay with her sad parents and overly critical crinkle-skinned grandparents on her un-wedding night; lies on creaky twin mattress between crispy sheets and

stares at ceiling for record 9.75 hours despite sleeping pill(s) that may or may not have been abused in excess and mixed with copious amounts of wine; begins un-honeymoon alone with largish hangover and shitty attitude.

No matter how the story starts, it's always the same: I am a loser with a horrible, losery life and negative thought process. My only real friend is my iPad, with which I write this loser blog diary that no one reads or even knows about. Am thinking seriously about giving up, buying a hypoallergenic cat, and becoming the token Elkton spinster.

Sigh.

Fact:
Not two days ago, Colin and I were snuggling on the couch, guzzling wine, and dreaming of a perfect future filled with wealth, fame, and sensual Jacuzzi whirlpool tubs despite a shared lack of overall talents and money-making skills. Colin was brainstorming on what we'd name our fictional future children if we were celebrities (girl = Freedom, boy = Carpet) and asked for my opinion on dancing down the aisle to Sir Mix-a-Lot's *Baby Got Back* following our first husband-and-wife kiss moment. After giving it some deep thoughts, I said that I was generally open to the idea, and we moved on to joke romantically about other things, all the while acting normally jolly and fine.

When I woke up the next morning, Colin – along with his phone charger, travel bag, and passport – was gone.

Who brings up Sir Mix-a-Lot and future celebrity offspring and then stands you up at your wedding the very next day? I'll tell you who: assholes. Assholes do that. Assholes also force you into going on your honeymoon alone, like you're a stupid, single, twenty-eight-year-old loser.

Blah.

So that's where this *un*-honeymoon blog diary officially begins:

approximately 32,000 feet in the air, on a crusty airplane en route to the tropical island of St. Thomas, where I am currently smooshed between two very fat people who are taking up more than half my seat with their slightly damp and generously odorous body parts.

To add insult to serious injury, aside from the obvious post-altar-dumpage depression, subsequent alcohol/sleeping pill abuse, the excruciatingly uncomfortable bed sheets that hadn't been washed since 1982, and my group of generally awful and unhelpful former friends, the whole start to my un-honeymoon has basically been comprised of one bad thing after another.

Starting, of course, with my parents' attempt to drive me to the airport.

"Turn there, Dad."

"Huh? Where? Where?" (Dad was incapable of driving while doing anything else, including talking and thinking.)

"Right there, Dad. Where it says 'Airport Drop Off.'"

"I don't see it. Where's da sign? I don't see it."

"Seriously, Dad, it's right there."

"Are you gonna be alright?" Mom was sporting red-rimmed, 'my-twenty-eight-year-old-daughter-was-just-dumped-on-her-wedding-day' eyes.

"Yes, Mom."

"I just think it's so brave dat yurr traveling alone. And yurr first time on a plane, how horrible."

"Stop crying, Mom. Please."

"It reminds me of dat girl from da TV who went to Bermuda and never came back. Just like dat. Dat's not where yurr headed, is it dear?"

"No, Mom. That was Aruba and it happened like ten years ago. I'm going to St. John. Dad, TURN HERE NOW."

"Has it been dat long already? Dale, did you know it's been ten whole years since dat girl from da TV went to Bermuda and never came back?"

"Ten years? Dat is a long time. A decade, even."

"Dad, you missed the turn!"

"What? What turn?"

"Aaaagh!"

"There's no need for dat sort of attitude, dear. Men like ladies, not negative ninnies. Here, I made you a Tubberware."

"Mom, I can't bring that through security. And no one says 'ninny' anymore. Dad, turn around right now."

"Where? Where should I turn around? Dis is all so confusing."

"It's hot dish. In da Tubberware. In case you get hungry on da airplane."

"Mom, please be quiet. Dad, pull over and let me drive."

"Pull over where?"

"Right here! Anywhere! Just do it! Aaagh!"

And so on.

I ended up being twenty minutes late for my first flight. Luckily, the flight had been delayed due to some scary dysfunctional plane wing issue, and I made it to the gate in the nick of time.

I had a brief moment of sanity en route to Charlotte because, luckily, the scary dysfunctional wing stayed intact the whole time. But then I somehow succeeded in grabbing the wrong carry-on bag as I got off the plane and was stuck waiting for the airport customer service loser squad to find my right bag for nearly forty-five minutes. Like any normal person, I was forced to take a whole Xanax just to make it through the situation in one piece.

When the airport customer service loser squad finally found my right bag, I had exactly eleven minutes to make it from one end of the Charlotte airport clear across to the other end. And those high-tech super cool time saving moving walkways that you always see functioning just fine in airports? Yeah, those were shut down for repair. All of them.

I had no choice but to sprint to my next gate in my new vacation flip flops while dragging my carry-on and purse behind me and acting generally wheezy and ridiculous.

By the time I got to the next gate, practically two whole miles from where I started, my connecting flight had already finished boarding and the following things had also happened:

1. I was pummeled by a bona fide asshole wearing a three piece, multi-thousand dollar suit complete with sparkly angel/devil cuff-links (stupid); fell on my butt, bruising both tailbone and wrist; rich man did not help me up but instead walked away like, well, an asshole. I subsequently lost all faith in the following things: equality, human rights, paying-it-forward, people-helping-people, Obamacare.

2. I had a total whack attack melt down in front of the customer service agent while begging her to let me on the plane so I wouldn't get stranded in the Charlotte airport like Tom Hanks in that movie where he has to live in the airport.

3. I broke my new vacation flip-flop strap and had to use my emergency duct tape to re-attach the strap; my new vacation flip-flop is now half flip-flop, half emergency duct tape. I officially believe I've been cursed. (Note to future self: figure out how to break curses.)

4. I began sweating heavily during the impromptu two-mile sprint across several airport zip codes and now smell noticeably like near-spoiled spinach. Both bosom and head remain abnormally sweaty.

Now that I've finally boarded, I'm pretty sure everyone on the plane blames me for the delay instead of blaming the stupid airline for misplacing my right bag in the first place and forcing me to run two miles between gates. I'm also pretty sure my row neighbors hate me and are purposely trying to smoosh me to death with their sticky skin folds.

In addition, the evil customer service lady forced-checked my travel bag so I now have no plane activities and am stuck staring at the back of a beige chair for the next four hours with only my iPad for company but no spare dollars in my travel budget with which to purchase overpriced airline Internet.

Sigh.

Anyway, I'm signing off to read a nasty airline magazine. (*Destination, U.S. Virgin Islands* – way out of date, but the only other option is a crusty *Skymall*.) I'll try not to think about how many disease-infested travelers touched this magazine before me. (Hundreds. Thousands. Infinity!)

Note to future self: always carry hand sanitizer. And deodorant.

Date: Sunday
Time: Just past noonish
Location: Worst moment of my life, except for yesterday.
Day Rating (So Far): Negative infinity stars.

Okay, I've definitely been cursed. I don't know how or why, but I have. I bet it was creepy Lena Olofsson who put the curse on me. There's always been something off about that girl, and she barely talked to me at the pretzel stand the other day! Plus I heard a rumor once that she was dating a Wiccan and the Wiccan taught her all about how to put curses on people. Now the whole entire world is busy laughing at me and my gullible loser dumbness. My emotional status has moved from self-deprecating to dangerously self-destructive. I currently feel that life is moderately horrendous; I want to crawl under the airplane seat and die.

Recap:
There I was, reading the diseased *Destination, U.S. Virgin Islands* magazine while generally minding my own business and attempting to ignore my warm smelly neighbors, when several things happened in a row, each exponentially worse than the thing before:

1. The pervy old man to my left rubbed my elbow and called me 'cowgirl.' He is currently breathing heavily into my hair and ear canal. I have no idea what to do so am choosing to pretend he is an invisible ghost-man. (Believe this is how most scary foreign horror films begin.)
2. The fat lady with chin hairs to my right sneezed all over my $8 airplane ham sando before I could take one bite. I haven't eaten a thing since dinner two nights ago and now have a sneezed-on-by-fat-stranger-with-chin-hairs sando sitting in front of me. Unfortunately, I am still thinking about eating it while

also second guessing my decision to leave Mom's hot dish Tubberware with airport security.

3. Update: lady and chin hairs have asked to eat contaminated ham sando. After some deliberation, I agreed.

And the worst – I repeat – *worst* thing of all:

4. I discovered that my jerk ex-fiancé is not only a complete and utter dick but is also a super-liar who lied about everything!

Let me back up.

Colin and I met about a year ago when I ended up at his fancy art gallery opening after coming off yet another blind date failure. That particular blind date disaster was named "Clem." Clem was about three inches shorter than me (I am 5'2" so...yeah). After realizing that his unfortunate height deficiency also came with premature baldness, poor conversing ability, and questionable job status, the entire blind date situation made me feel like crawling out a window and running away as fast as possible. To die.

A friend of my then-roommate knew Colin, who was, according to the friend, so nervous about his first gallery opening that he forced everyone in the tri-state area to attend and pretend to be interested in buying things. Colin's theory was that the real potential buyers, after seeing so much fake interest in the art, would be much more likely to buy something. (I actually think this is a great theory and is probably how most infomercials work.)

When I called my roommate after deciding to bail on my bald pocket-date during his fourth trip to the bathroom, she invited me to carpool with her to wherever this gallery event was taking place. I figured that feigning interest in crappy art to help mentally judo someone else into buying it sounded much better than listening to my pocket-date describe his mother's collection of antique china dolls, especially the doll she believed was possessed by the spirit of her dead 'Pop Pop'. So I went.

Colin liked my thin lips, huge forehead, and ability to act overly enthusiastic about crappy art stuff. I liked his largish nose and floppy hair and how he didn't live in Elkton like all the other losers I know.

We'd both dated less attractive people before so proceeded to spend the whole rest of the night getting very drunk on expensive champagne while discussing our shared love of sensual Jacuzzi whirlpool tubs. Then we were a couple, just like that, and I happily broke my two-year-unintentional-sex-hiatus. In general, our relationship was great most of the time. Or some of the time. At least.

A few months in, I learned through reading his mail that Colin rented an inspirational artist's loft on the tropical island of St. Thomas because the view was 'muse-ical.' (His joke, not mine. Thank God.) (PS – I guess you say *on* instead of *in* when referring to islands because you can't really be *in* an island. Physically, I mean. Unless you're in a volcano or cave, I guess. Anyway…)

I wasn't that pissed when I found out that Colin had a mysterious tropical getaway. In fact, I thought it was sort of great. I *was* pissed that he was trying to hide this amazing getaway from me though. I mean, I had to find out about it by going through his mail. I suppose it's not really the sort of thing that comes up in conversation that often, but he should have told me about it anyway (dick!) and then taken me there immediately.

Around the same time, I also discovered that Colin had some mysterious credit issues due to some mysterious identity theft scenario a few years back and was subsequently prohibited from buying anything of consequence or even renting a car.

Of course, I should have taken these mysterious discoverings as the cautionary signs they ended up being but, instead, I was love-blinded by Colin's nice floppy hair and his unique artist/hipster coolness. I figured, like an idiot, that it would be a wonderful idea to purchase an over-budget townhouse so we could live there together and party epically in our sensual Jacuzzi whirlpool tub.

(By the way, Colin's judo mind tricks during his gallery thing did actually pay off, and he sold loads of art and made loads of money. So he did pay for some of the things in our new townhouse…like the sensual Jacuzzi tub installation, for example, and our new wall-to-wall non-shag carpeting. This generally made me feel like I was way richer than I actually am. So, naturally, I blame the whole entire thing on him.)

Anyway, about six months after we moved in together, I came across a ring in Colin's bureau while putting his laundry away and looking through his things. It was a slightly odd looking non-diamond ring with a red stone where the regular diamond should have been and a very antique looking silver ring setting. It was slightly too small for my finger and definitely highly non-diamondy in character. When I asked Colin about it (I mean, when he walked in when I was holding it and going through his things), he went very sheepish and cute and got down on one knee and asked me to marry him! That's when he told me he'd designed the non-diamond ring himself, spending months and months utilizing his creative and artistic prowess while simultaneously pouring his heart and soul into creating the most perfect ring known to (wo)man.

I was so excited to not only be engaged to a bona fide artist/jewelry maker but to also possess a super amazing, super unique, nothing-like-it-in-the-whole-entire-world engagement ring. Oh, the looks on my un-friends' faces when I told them it was a one-of-a-kind and not taken out of some secondhand pawn shop like Melody's or posted up on the Jewelry Barn billboard next to the Fleet Farm like Amanda's!

The whole thing was just so romantic and amazing and, like an idiot, I thought the romantic amazingness would last forever.

It did not.

Now that everyone is up to speed on my relationship, or lack thereof, with my assholio ex-fiancé, let me ask you this:

If your fiancé spent months and months designing a piece of crap non-diamond engagement ring and commissioning a top-crap-non-diamond-ring-designer to make it specially unique and one-of-a-kind-like then why the **MOTHER FUCK** is that same exact ring advertised for sale in some random crusty airline magazine?!?!?!

GRRRRRR!!!!!

Life is the pits! I'm officially the biggest, most gullible loser in the entire world. Stupid curse.

It doesn't help that the ring on my finger and the ring in the magazine ad are 100 percent identical and that, for some idiot reason, I didn't leave my ring at home before embarking on this stupid trip in the first place. It's currently sitting on my finger, looking all garish and non-diamondy, and non-unique at all. A 3.03 carat round brilliant red stone set in a hexagonal frame with a hand-engraved filigree crown, as advertised by Sapphire Junction, the hottest St. Thomas jewelry store sensation. *Stop in Today!* and all that crap.

That stupid, lying ass!

Now I'm bawling my eyes out, getting my wireless keyboard dangerously wet, and scaring my fat neighbors into thinking I'm some sort of odd airplane loser who cries at magazine advertisements. I was absolutely forced to take another half-Xanax just to make it through the situation in one piece.

This was the worst idea in the history of all ideas. I couldn't possibly be more upset with Dad and his "go find your smile" speech and sad swimmy eye tricks. No one goes to a tropical romantic island *alone*! What am I going to do the whole time, anyway? Swim in the ocean by myself? Go to the bar by myself and watch everyone else make out? Sightsee by myself? Like some dumb loser?

I've officially followed through on the worst idea of all time. When I arrive on St. Thomas, I am getting the first flight back home, pawning my losery un-special ring, and moving on with my life.

Stupid vacations, stupid airplanes, stupid lying non-ring designing dicks!

Date: Sunday
Time: Unsure as time change is a bit confusing, and also had mucho alcohol accidentally (on purpose).
Location: Island taxi cab, en route to a mysterious tropical island place called the Red Hook ferry dock.
Day Rating (So Far): Medium.

Let me set one thing straight: Colin and I are no longer a couple, right? I mean, when a stupid un-fiancé with credit issues no-shows your wedding, doesn't answer your hundreds of phone calls, lies about designing your un-special engagement ring, and makes you go on a solo honeymoon disaster, it means you're broken up, right? I guess I've never read the official rules on un-spoken breakups but I'm writing it down in this blog diary to let it be known that, in my book (blog diary), Colin and I are 100 percent broken up. Definitively.

Now that we've made that clear and avoided any future misunderstandings, let me share the most magical thing that's just happened.

I've met a guy.

Not just *a* guy. A hottie. A complete and total sexy-cute, broad shouldered, nice-butted, tropical island future-fling-potential *hot*-tie. And he's absolutely, definitely interested in me! (I'm not quite sure why, but he is. I think.)

Hurrah! Life is so grand and filled with wonderful tropical island surprises!

Recap:

When the plane finally landed *on* St. Thomas, I stumbled onto the sizzling tarmac in a daze. My ears were ringing from the demon child sitting directly behind me who decided to have a multi-hour whack attack that included: screaming, banging, spitting, crying, and lots and lots of seat kicking. I found out later that the demon child belonged to none other than my sneezy, chin haired, ham sando stealing neighbor. I was not surprised.

I was so pissed at the demon child and her super gross mother that I nearly forgot all about the ring ad, which I totally ripped out of the magazine and stuffed into my purse so I could go back and look at it and cry some more later. Unfortunately, I only managed to rip out half of the page because a stewardess came by and scared me into thinking I was doing something super illegal and property damaging. But I got the good half of the ad, anyway. The part with the picture of the ring. And, after I sped-walked far away from the chin-haired sando stealer and her misbehaving offspring, I did eventually remember the half-ad sitting there in my purse, waiting for me to clutch it to my chest and cry hormonally for hours. And then I got even more upset than I already was.

Like any normal person, I was forced to take another half-Xanax to make it through the whole thing without dying.

The best thing about the St. Thomas airport was the free rum station on the way to baggage claim. The line was way too long though so, naturally, I used my small stature to my advantage and budged in front to grab a shot (or two) of yummy island rum.

After I elbowed my way through the crowd to enter the damp and slightly foul smelling baggage claim area, I immediately noticed two more most glorious things:

1. A shitty overpriced snack bar!
Hurrah! I hadn't eaten anything in twoish days and was beginning to worry about a potential self-cannibalism situation. I didn't even mind that three rubbery chicken strips and soggy fries cost $10.99. Any food was better than eating my own stomach lining, spendy faux chicken included.

2. Magical life-saving alcohol bar!
Hurrah! More alcohol! I hadn't had anything to drink in twoish minutes and was beginning to feel suicidally depressed about everything in my life in general. I didn't even mind that one Red Stripe cost $7.00; it was much better than losing a battle with the army of suicidally depressing thoughts dancing around in my brain.

So I made myself at home at the bar and ordered a Red Stripe, fully intending to break all of my un-honeymoon not-to-do-rules.

(By the way, just so everyone knows, drinking while on Xanax is very unsafe and generally not recommended at all, under any circumstance. I only do it because I'm overly depressed and self-destructive, and also because it makes me feel super awesome and great. Don't do it.)

Anyway, there I was in my duct-taped vacation flip flops, torn blue jeans, smelly gray t-shirt, comfy travel hoodie (complete with armpit-hole), and faded gray Castro hat, busy inhaling greasy snack bar food like a starved lioness while mixing alcohol with prescription medication. I was fully ready to grab my bag and figure out how to purchase an overly expensive flight back home with my already maxed out credit card (realizing that, in order to make it back home, I'd probably have to stoop to horrible new lows and call my parents for funds). I decided I might as well get good and drunk first, to ease the horror of it all.

Then, it happened.

The Time I Met My Future Potential Island Fling for the First Time

(The following is a 100 percent accurate reenactment of the first ever conversation I had with my future potential island fling.)

Me: Sitting there minding my own business, drinking my beer, getting chicken strips all over my face, and being generally depressed and disgusting.
Hottie: "Can I get you another one?"
Me: "Huh?"
Hottie: Sits down on the stool next to me.
Me (taking inventory): Blue gray eyes, light brown hair with sexy blondish highlights, heart melting dimples (plural), oh-so-broad shoulders, pec-hugging soft looking t-shirt, oh the biceps, the floppy hair – don't look at his lap, do not look at his lap. Oh *God* – a wonderful, beautiful lap bulge. This is not happening. This absolutely cannot be happening!
Hottie: "Can I get you another beer?"
Me (to myself): Ohmigod, he's actually talking to me. Crap! I look horrible! This never happens to people like me and, now that it's actually happening, it's at the worst possible time on the worst possible day at the worst possible moment! Now he's staring at me! He thinks I'm special needs! Crap! Say something! Anything! Anything at all!
Me: "Uh – um…um, sure. I guess. I mean, thanks." (Idiot! Worst response ever!)

Hottie: "I'm Shane."
Me (Paraphrasing): More awful, awkward things. Blah blah. I'm from Minnesota! Land of 10,000 lakes! Mall of America!
Shane (Paraphrasing): I'm heading to St. John too. Great minds and other clichés. I'm super cute and sexy simultaneously. I have a strong relationship with my mother. I'm a writer from Philadelphia doing a story on sensual tropical islands; let's flirt and have tons of travel fun!
Me: "Definitely! Sounds great! Let me drink this other beer first. Because I just had like five Xanax and getting drunk while on Xanax is definitely not going to be a problem at all."
Shane: "Want to share a taxi to the ferry and be together forever, until we go back to our non-island lives?"
(At this point, Shane started staring and re-staring at my engagement ring, acting generally confused and very attractive.)
Me: "Wonderful! I'm definitely not married. I just wear this ring for fun, so, like, no worries. Oh where's my travel bag? I lost it *again*! Oh nooo!"
Shane: "Don't worry. I, Shane, will find it."
Me: "You're the best! Your dimples are super."
Shane: "I know. Be right back."

Okay, so it didn't happen *exactly* like that, but you get the gist.

Anyway, while my new island sex hunk was off looking for my elusive carry-on that had somehow not yet made its way into the baggage claim area, I made the mistake of opening my compact and seeing the horrors of post-altar-dumpage, no-pre-shower traveling, Xanax/alcohol bloatedness, and general insomnia.

I technically looked so horrible that I worried Shane might be a fiction of my Xanax/alcohol hallucinogenic imagination. I mean, in what world does a perfect ten decide to walk up to a six (five), buy her a beer at a seedy airport baggage claim bar, and act all cute and flirty and wonderful? Especially when the six (five) has stray pieces of hair stuck to her greasy forehead and bits of fried chicken strip on her chin. It didn't seem right. Especially considering the curse I had on me.

Shane found my travel bag a few minutes later, and we decided to order another round of beers. Things were going great, aside from the fact that Shane seemed a little wary about my wearing an engagement ring and flirting with him at the same time. I didn't mind, obviously, because of his cute butt and other areas, and we continued to flirt heavily for quite some time. After awhile, I forgot all about my plan to call my parents, beg for funds, and head back home. Shane was making my lower belly region go all warm and flushy, and all I wanted to do was jump on his lap and force him to have sex with me over and over again until the end of time.

After we finished our beers, which Shane paid for like a bona fide island fling candidate, we decided to catch a taxi van to the Red Hook ferry dock. Together. At present, we are sharing our taxi van with five other travelers who are all very drunk and slurring on about the storm that may or may not hit the islands tonight. I'm attempting to avoid drunken-travelers-breath while reading Shane's furious text messagings over his shoulder. So far, I've only caught bits of words – *eye* and *break* and other things. I'm pretty certain he's breaking up with the non-island girlfriend he definitely has so that he and I can have mucho sex and other things and I can show Colin just how fast I can get over his lying losery ass.

Once Shane and I cruise across the ocean and dock on St. John, we will surely become a tied-at-the-hip travel couple. I'll spend the rest of my un-honeymoon having lots of delicious morning sex instead of watching sunsets by myself and crying into my beach rum. Hurrah!

Okay, I'm signing off since we should be nearly to Red Hook by now. I also think the drunkish traveling man next to me is reading this blog diary entry and both analyzing and judging me. I'm thoroughly creeped out and also beginning to feel a bit vomitous from the curvy streets and alcohol/Xanax abuse.

Date: Sunday
Time: Three-ish p.m.
Location: St. John Cruz Bay Ferry Dock.
Day Rating (So Far): A highly bipolar and emotionally complex one star.

Remember when I warned you about mixing Xanax and alcohol because you might embarrass yourself in front of a sexycute-rippling-bicep-future-island-fling-hottie? I hope you took that seriously. I know I didn't.

By the time the taxi dropped us off and our drunken traveling squad somehow made it onto the St. John-bound ferry, it was pouring rain and I was a wet, wasted mess. I honestly didn't mean to accidentally overdose. It just sort of happened. Like when one just sort of happens to eat an entire box of Oreo cookies while watching *Love Actually* and feeling very bad about the state of one's hair and skin.

After boarding, Shane helped me onto a ferry bench. I was so busy feeling queasy and awful I could barely even enjoy all the wonderful things that were happening. Like seeing the ocean for the very first time in my whole life. Or the sexy muscled arm Shane wrapped around my shoulder in an attempt to keep me upright. Or the up-close experience with a very soft and good smelling t-shirt.

Because I am a major loser who messes up absolutely everything in my life, I passed out on Shane's shoulder within three minutes of sitting down. Aaagh! I fully blame the too-soft t-shirt, recent insomnia, and over-indulgence in chicken strips. Even though it was most likely my total inability to handle medium substance abuse.

By the time I woke up – not even a half hour later – I was seeing double and battling both vertigo and sea sickness. And Shane was nowhere to be found.

Yep. I lost my island hottie. Just like that. Life went from crap to rainbow to crap all in the same hour. In an alternate life, I would check into *Celebrity Rehab*, go into the little room where one speaks with the camera, and cry about how I only wanted to be a good mother to Freedom and Carpet and how I didn't mean to mix the this with the that and to make sure to read my tell-all book coming to virtual book stores near you, just in time for the holidays.

After the ferry docked and everyone else debarked, one of the poor ferry workers had to nudge me awake. I'm pretty sure he had to nudge me a few times. Or a lot of times.

Once awake, I stumbled out onto the ferry dock, onto the island of St. John, out into the warmish and actually kind of nice rain, completely and utterly alone. Like a totally un-honeymoonish, accidental-almost-overdosage, super small-town loser.

Fucking great.

After the ferry dudes unloaded everyone's luggage, and I finally re-located my ever-elusive travel bag, I called René, the caretaker of the villa Colin had rented (and pre-paid for, thank God). The villa was owned by the friend of someone Colin had worked with or something like that and was generally very mysterious and super discounted. I'm not really sure how it all came to be. In any case, René said to wait for her at the ferry dock so she could pick me up and bring me to the travel car place. So that is what I'm doing.

Since I have nothing to do while waiting for René and have no island sex god to distract me with his flirty laugh and perfectly chiseled features, I figured I would hide out under the little ferry dock overhang and engage in some serious multi-tasking, including: updating my blog diary, watching all the happier tourists being all dumb and happy, pondering my recent life events, and becoming ultra learned and cultured about tropical islands.

Good plan.

Time: Three-tenish p.m.

Okay, here is what I have learned from my multi-tasking so far:

1. Everyone is part of a good-looking couple or family, except me. I am literally the only solo person on this whole dumb island. Super dumb.
2. Everyone is all kissy-face with everyone else and acting super dumb and overly affectionate about everything.

3. Everyone drives a Jeep Wrangler. And by everyone, I mean all the people. There are no other vehicles except for Jeep Wranglers. Even though I've only been on the island for like five seconds, I've already seen the following Jeep Wrangler colors: neon green, neon orange, hot pink, jet black, sea foam green, peach pastel, egg-shell blue, matte, high-gloss, glittery, non-glittery, chrome rims, black rims, et cetera and so on. It's like watching a traveling rainbow, and I'm very confused on what to look at. (I wonder how all the Jeep Wranglers made it to this little island in the middle of nowhere. Was there like a floating Jeep parade that happened?)

4. Everyone looks way too happy – all tanned and glowy and smiling, like a bunch of stupid dumb losers. I desperately want to be like those happy glowy couples, and I never, ever want to go back to a place where sixteen inches of snow and negative thirty degree temperatures are considered normal.

Stupid island.

Time: Three-twentyish p.m.

So...instead of doing the rest of the multi-tasking I was supposed to be doing, I might have definitely spent the last ten minutes wallowing about being dumped and lied to and losing my stupid island sex god.

Marrying Colin was my way out, okay? Fine. I admit it. It was my only way out of stupid Elkton. First of all, who lives in a town called Elkton? I'll tell you who: assholes. Assholes live in places called Elkton. Ooh, a town filled with elk and elk farmers and elk processing factories and people who love elk. Coool. Not.

In reality, Elkton is just a stupid dumb place with our dumb Super Walmart and our dumb meat packing plant that exports stupid elk and other questionable meat products. Everyone knows everyone and talks about everyone behind their backs and gossip spreads faster than an undesirable skin rash.

Colin was a world traveler with a mysterious secret artist's quarters and a strong side profile. He designed unique artsy things that people actually kind of liked, sometimes. Plus he had a 4.3 star rating on his Etsy store and had a desperate and very endearing love for sushi and other high-class things.

Sure, he had credit card/identity theft issues and couldn't rent a car. Sure, he traveled a ton and didn't really call me a lot when he was gone. Sure, he used really embarrassing words, like 'zafty' and 'housecoat.' And sure, he had a very real and intense case of lethophobia (which basically means he was afraid of oblivion, I think, or something similarly cultured and deep). But he was generally very nice and sweet, and I really did love his strong side profile.

Plus, I thought he actually cared about me, dammit, and would one day sweep me off my feet and whisk me away to someplace exotic and amazing to live a way better, way more exciting and artistic life with him.

Of course he wouldn't actually care about me. Who would? I'm boring little Sammy Stone from stupid Loserville, Minnesota. I have boring friends who are only my friends because we have been friends since diapers and can walk to each others' houses.

In addition, I have a positively horrid job in Human Resources working for the elk factory, a truly disgusting position where I am required to maintain the employee handbook and have regular conversations with elk and elk-related factory workers about appropriate workplace behaviors. I have my very own pint-sized cubicle, an annual salary just below the poverty line, and a demon boss named Kelly. (Who is a guy. Named Kelly. Just making that clear. It seems there used to be a lot of guys named Kelly, but you don't really hear it much now. We call him Kelly Smelly behind his back. And by we, I mean me, Sally from the mail room, Maude the office manager who is, in fact, as ancient as her name implies, and Eric Lang the all-rounder. It's really fucking sad, you know. Kelly doesn't even smell. He's just so horrible and it's the only thing we could think of that rhymed with Kelly.)

Most of the time, I just want to crawl under my little cubicle desk and die.

In fact, updating my new blog diary is really the only thing I look forward to doing at all. Of course, no one reads it or knows I exist. I only do it because it's way cheaper than therapy and because it helps me fight off the soul-crushing boredom that comes with living in a town like Elkton.

Anyway, it's finally stopped raining. I'm going to go walk around for a bit and see what's so great about this stupid tropical island. Hopefully René hasn't forgotten about me.

Time: Three-twenty-twoish p.m.
Location: St. John Cruz Bay Boardwalk

Hmmm...there seems to be one unhappy not-in-love couple on this dumb island. I wanted to pop over to the Beached Bar and get an island rum to tide me over until René picked me up, but instead I'm watching a tall gorgeous man with black hair argue with a tall gorgeous woman with brown hair. Right in front of the Beached Bar. Right in front of everyone. I'm going to try to get a little closer to figure out what they're fighting about.

Time: Three-twenty-threeish p.m.

Never mind. They saw me coming and left. Crap. Didn't they know that listening to their argument was probably going to be the highlight of my un-honeymoon? Lame.

Time: Fiveish
Location: St. John Nast-hole Villa.

Since following Shane to St. John despite my plans to return home immediately, I have to admit that being on St. John sort of made me feel like I'd just stepped into the tropical postcard hanging up on my fridge at home. Maybe this island wasn't so lame after all. In fact, it's probably the most beautiful place I've ever seen in my life. With its clear turquoise water and lush green trees and tropical flowers and the sweet, slightly salty smell of the breeze. Even though I had been dumped at the altar and had a super bad attitude about it, I was lucky. Luckier than a lot of people who never got the opportunity to travel to an exotic tropical island...alone.

Plus, I've already seen multiple oceanside bars advertising never-ending happy hour specials and lots of oceanside shops advertising lots of interesting looking things. There's even a real live boardwalk! I've always wanted to walk on one of those.

After seeing the bars and the shops and the real live boardwalk (and the entertaining arguing couple), I decided that maybe this whole un-honeymoon idea wasn't so horrible after all. In fact, I was actually quite looking forward to getting to my island villa and taking an amazingly incredible, super hot and refreshing shower before enjoying one of the many tropical island happy hours.

I really shouldn't have been so excited.

When René finally showed up at the ferry dock, she and I went to pick up my Jeep Wrangler – a foxy, slate colored sex kitten, a.k.a. my perfect vacation fully-insured-to-the-max vehicle. Then we headed to my villa – her in her Jeep, me in mine. I followed her out of Cruz Bay, right through a stop sign I didn't see, and straight up a long windy hill called Jacob's Ladder.

Just so you know, everyone drives on the left side of the road on St. John. People tell you this multiple times when you pick up the rental car. There are also lots of very distracting bright yellow stickers that scream "Stay Left! LEFT! LEFT!" posted all over the dashboard and steering wheel. St. John is somehow technically still America (which is all very confusing), so I'm not really sure why everyone drives on the left. I heard it's because someone built the roads wrong, but that doesn't really make much sense to me. Aren't they the same on both sides?

In any case, I adapted to left-lane driving like a total pro. This made me feel very 007 and mission-capable, and I eventually had the grand idea to figure out where Colin's stupid island loft was so I could go pay him a visit. Then I could yell/sob at him in person instead of on his voicemail.

(Note to future self: think more on how to act during potential Colin reunion: perhaps either cold and sexy or confident and hard-to-get. Also: think more like 007. Also: learn to shoot gun like 007.)

Anyway, René drove me to the villa and walked me inside, talking in super-hyper-mode the whole time. She was very short like me but had very brown skin, long brown hair, brown eyes, and a winning attitude. She may have been on drugs.

Once inside, René made a bunch of circles on some maps, shoved two keys in my face, joked about the dead plants littering the balcony, showed me where the flashlights were (please God, may I never have reason to use those flashlights), and turned on a dusty, nasty floor fan. Then she left.

At present, I am completely alone in a massive villa with two bedrooms, two bathrooms, a ginormous kitchen, granite everything, and a bona fide wraparound balcony porch that overlooks Cruz Bay and its postcard-worthy turquoise ocean. Yes, it's actually turquoise! Like in the pictures!

The wraparound balcony comes complete with a table, two chairs, a tiki bar, and a weird closet thing on one side with a rusty washer and dryer and some moldy swim gear, like flippers and one of those…water mask things. I'm not really sure what I'm supposed to do with all that. Otherwise, the balcony is really great. Sort of bird-poop filled…and the tiki bar is sort of moldy and devoid of all alcohol, and the chairs are sort of crusty looking…but otherwise, it's okay. I guess.

Unfortunately, due to the sweltering tropical temperatures and the villa's total lack of air conditioning, it is practically 1,000 degrees inside the villa. My fingers are sweating and making my fancy wireless keyboard very squishy. In addition, there is loud, annoying construction going on next door, the floor is littered with tiny dead bug carcasses, and I am already so bored I'm about to die (even though I have only been here for like 20 minutes). The only positive is the free wireless Internet. At least I can watch my *America's Next Top Model* episodes thanks to Amazon Prime.

Oh – also, there's no hot water.

I repeat: no hot water. None. Zip. Zilch. Zero. Only cold water here, folks. I learned this while attempting to wash a dirty plate that was left in the sink from some former resident and/or homeless person.

If I were a braver woman, I'd call René and force her to come back and fix the hot water and dirty sweaty dead bug issues immediately but, truth is, I lack both courage and eloquence and generally avoid confrontation at all costs. Plus, she's obviously the crappiest caretaker in the whole world, and I am the unlucky benefactor. Fabulous.

I guess I'm off to take the *not*-amazingly incredible *not*-super hot shower I was so looking forward to.

Welcome to my stupid un-honeymoon.

Date: Sunday
Time: Post-excruciatingly-cold-shower
Location: Beached Bar.
Day Rating (So Far): Zero stars on my way to deliciously drunk.

The best thing about St. John so far is the sheer number of super yummy glowy island gods. The male/female ratio is most definitely in my favor, and I have already been hit on by two real non-pervy men!

The first non-perv was Shane, obviously, but since he ditched me on the ferry, I'm really not sure that I'll ever see him again. He probably realized I was a random drunken stranger with alcohol control issues and took the opportunity to run away as fast as possible as soon as possible. He may have even decided to jump overboard and swim for shore, to make his getaway faster.

The second non-perv's name is Jimmy (lol, I know). Jimmy has sexy green eyes, longish black hair that does a little curl at the bottom, and super amazing bartending skills. I'm pretty sure Jimmy was the male half of the arguing couple I saw earlier, but I don't want to ask and embarrass him. Hopefully that gorgeous woman he was yelling at wasn't his girlfriend. I'm going to pretend it wasn't.

I am currently at the Beached Bar, my first ever bar on the wonderful, glorious island of St. John. I'm staring at the turquoise ocean, pretending not to notice all the happy newly wedded couples all around me, and enjoying one of Jimmy's delightful concoctions, aptly called a Painkiller. This may be my second or third Painkiller. Not sure, don't care.

Jimmy has already asked me many interesting things about myself and seems generally very interested in all the interesting things I have to say.

Life is once again lovely and filled with many wonderful green-eyed, long-lashed opportunities!

Date: Sun
Time: Partee!
Location: St. John the best so far.
Day Rating: Infinite.

Yesss! Herr I am, on toilet. Figured all out you see. Now know evrything.

Whatever you say, do not forget about me. in toilet.

Date: Monday morn
Time: Four-ish blurry
Location: Villa bathroom floor.
Day Rating (So Far): Worst yet.

Oh God, oh holy God. Oh it's spinning. Everything is spinning. Stupid Painkillers and your delicious candy flavor. Why did I have to drink you so much? You've only made me feel vomitous and horrible.

I have zero clue how I made it back to the villa in one piece. I woke up in bed, thankfully alone, thankfully clothed (although disastrously sans underpants), with a big hole in my memory where the night used to be. Now I'm curled up on the cold bathroom floor alternating between sobs and barfing. I feel disgustingly depressed with a woefully small confidence level. All I want to do is to curl up under something stationary and die.

What I Remember About Last Night

1. I went to the Beached Bar after my excruciatingly painful, ice-cold, non-relaxing vacation shower. (However, the cold shower water successfully made my hair shiny and great for the first time ever, so perhaps evil shower is not so bad after all.)

2. I ordered a beachy rum cocktail from Jimmy, the sexy green-eyed, black haired hottie bartender who stared at my un-engagement ring with a horrible expression on his face like I was some sort of finger leper. (I must remember to search for a villa safe in which to leave my ring for the remainder of my holiday so as not to scare off potential non-pervy island flings.)

3. Discovered that Painkillers taste like coconut and dreams. Successfully drank first Painkiller in under one minute.

4. Ordered Painkiller #2, to which Jimmy added a complimentary cherry because he obviously thought I was amazing and wonderful and mysteriously Midwestern. Jimmy made conversation by asking me where I was staying and other interesting details. I became so distracted by his long dark eyelashes that I drank Painkiller #2 in under one minute.

5. After Painkiller #2, my hottie-island-future-fling, Shane, reappeared out of thin air like Harry Houdini put together! I was instantly happier than I've ever been and was back to feeling wonderful about all things in general. Minus the wedding-dumpage and missing ex-fiancé, of course.

6. Shane acted way sexier and way more into me than before he ditched me on the ferry. His excuse for ditching me on the ferry involved a former coworker, a long-time-no-see situation, an ensuing difficult-to-get-away-from discussion, and so on. I mostly believed him but was too busy drinking my third Painkiller and enjoying thoughts of juggling two island men to care.

7. Shane ordered Cherry Bomb #1 and we toasted "to new adventures." I thought this was hilarious because Sammy Stone and adventures do not mix, at all. Ever. Period.

8. Cherry Bomb #1 tasted like candied unicorn tears and caused both immediate drunkage and permanent short-term memory loss.

There it is. That's all I remember about the entire night. It may or may not have stormed, I may or may not have done something completely ridiculous and embarrassing, and I most definitely scared Shane off for the rest of my life for being the drunk passing out girl twice in one day. I hope to God that Shane and my missing underpants have absolutely nothing in common.

I've officially become that horribly annoying person who can't hold her liquor but keeps on drinking anyway. Excuse me while I go barf and pass out on this nice, cool bathroom tile.

Date: Monday morn, continued
Time: Eightish
Location: Ripped-apart villa.
Day Rating (So Far): Worse than before. Way infinity worse.

Crap!!! Crap, crap, crap!

Crap!!!!

Why does every single thing in my stupid dreadful life have to go from generally awful to fucking disaster practically every single day? Can I just get a break, for once? Please? Damn you Lena Olofsson and all your weird personality traits and your supreme Wiccan knowledge on how to put curses on people. Why me? What did I ever do to you?

(Note to future self: figure out how to break curses; find island sorceress or similar and ask about breaking curses; Google curse-breaking ideas; do all the ideas.)

There I was, passed out on the bathroom floor and generally minding my own business when I woke up feeling much less nauseated but incredibly dehydrated and a little empty on the inside. I didn't notice anything wrong at first except for a generally odd feeling that something wasn't quite right. I chalked the feeling up to (1) being a drunken embarrassment in front of Shane, *again*, and (2) general uneasiness re: losing my underpants.

I got up and hobbled into the kitchen to drink the gallon of water that someone had graciously left in the fridge. I also noticed that the fridge contained: a half empty bottle of Chardonnay, a crumpled paper bag from an island restaurant called 'St. John Sushi,' a wedge of Swiss cheese, and a withered apple. (The whole unwashed, crusty food filled villa situation is highly confusing but my brain is too cloudy right now to even think about it.)

My stomach went all sloshy and uncomfortable due to the extreme water intake, and the only thing in the world I wanted to do was pop a dozen Advil and sleep for infinity more hours.

I crawled into my sweltering, 1,000 degree bed and stared at the ceiling, wondering why I felt like I'd forgotten something important, like turning my cubicle space heater off before leaving work so it exploded and is now burning all of Elkton to a crisp. Or something similar.

Then, I figured it out.

Remember my ring? My engagement ring? The ring that has given me nothing but trouble since the very first time I laid eyes on it? The ring I never should have brought to my stupid un-honeymoon in the first place? The ring I thought was amazingly special and one-of-a-kind-like but later found out was a crappy, un-special island tourist ring currently on clearance at a tropical island jewelry shop? The one I was planning to sell to Gary from New to You, Elkton's sleazy pawn shop? (FYI - Gary offered me five thousand dollars for it when he heard Colin and I split. Five thousand dollars! That's three months of mortgage payments on the over-budget townhouse that I'm dangerously close to defaulting on. I need that money like now!)

Yeah. That ring is 100 percent utterly and completely gone.

Gonzo. Not on my finger. Not on my person. Not in the villa. Not anywhere. I've gone and lost it. Like a stupid, unlucky drunk loser.

How am I going to make my next mortgage payment, due in two weeks' time? I'll be forced to foreclose on my townhouse, declare bankruptcy, and move in with my parents. Then, I'll have an enormous nervous breakdown and go on a newsworthy shooting spree after stripping off my clothes and dancing naked through the streets of Elkton for everyone to see.

On top of all that, the naked shooting spree will probably end with my arrest and a new free home in a federal penal colony. A penal colony filled wall-to-wall with sex-hungry lesbians. I won't last one day with those lesbians! I'll get nervous and drop the soap and my life will be over! It's all so horrible. All because I didn't leave my stupid non-diamond un-engagement ring at home.

Fucking great.

Date: Monday
Time: Post missing ring whack attack
Location: Ripped-apart villa.
Day Rating (So Far): Less than the worst thing you could possibly imagine.

The whack attack I was having over my missing ring and sudden loss of short-term financial security was temporarily put on hold by a knock at the front door. I desperately hoped the porch dweller would be a glowy island sex god and have in hand: my missing purse, Jeep keys, $5,000 un-engagement ring, and underpants. I momentarily lost myself in dreams of recovering my missing possessions while inviting the doorstep dwelling muscled man into my sweltering villa for some water and morning sex. I ended up being only partially right.

When I opened the door, in danced the most horribly gorgeous woman I'd ever seen in real life. I hated her immediately.

"I've brought your bag," she called as I shut the door behind her, like she was Queen of the Island and I was her personal slave.

It was raining again, and the evil gorgeous bitch dragged in pools of water that puddled all over the floor, and she didn't even notice or apologize one bit. (Why is it that beautiful people can get away with being rude and self-centered and generally amazing? Note to future self: be more like her immediately.)

I followed her into the kitchen, trying to figure out if we knew each other and re-thinking my decision to let her into the villa. As I watched her shake off her spendy-looking raincoat and inspect her spendy-looking island shoes, I started feeling highly aware of my general lack of physical attractiveness and spendy-looking wardrobe.

"Why is it so damn hot in here?" the woman asked, glaring at me.

"There's no AC," I replied cautiously.

"Well turn on a floor fan or something," she said. "My God."

"Do we...?" She looked so familiar, but I couldn't place her. My brain was too cloudy and my emotional status too bruised. Thinking was painful. I wanted to go lay down again.

Then I noticed she was holding my purse, thank *God*. I tried not to notice that the bag was soaking wet and dripping all over the floor. I hoped all my travel documents were intact.

"You don't remember me, do you?"

I shook my head and the woman laughed, shaking her head back at me, her stupid gorgeous hair looking all shiny and great.

"You were more out of it than I thought!" she said, walking into the bathroom and helping herself to a white fluffy towel.

I started hating her more.

The woman proceeded to tell me the following things that I half-listened to as I dug through my soggy purse in hopes of recovering my missing ring/underpants/car keys: her name was Leah, she was originally from Virginia but moved to St. John four years ago to open a spa, she visited the Beached Bar every Sunday night to dance the salsa, and saw me making sexy eyes at her boyfriend, Jimmy.

Damn.

"Don't worry," she said. "I wasn't jealous or anything. I mean..."

Offense taken.

"Seriously, don't worry about it," Leah said. "He's sexy, I know."

Dead sexy. Yes, I agree. Lucky bitch.

"And the eyes, so green."

Yes. Green eyes. Very green.

"So what if he's a bartender, right?"

"What?" I asked. "What's wrong with being a bartender?"

"What's *not* wrong with being a bartender?"

"Um..." I stammered. Did she want me to answer that? I tried to think. "Um...the hours?" I said finally.

"Never mind." She rolled her eyes, sighing. "There's just...the *je ne sais quoi*," she sighed again. "So much."

"What?"

Leah looked at me like I was an idiot just because I didn't know her stupid foreign phrases.

"The *je ne sais quoi*," she said. "You know."

Right.

(Note to future self: Google that.)

Apparently, while Leah made sure I didn't make a move on her boyfriend, she also noticed I was making sexy eyes at most of the bar-goers while dancing in a slightly awkward non-salsa fashion with Shane all night. Crap. (My feelings of drunken horror have increased exponentially. It's official. I've once again ruined any island romance potential due to my inability to dance properly and handle alcohol of any kind.)

Late in the night, after I had plenty of time to do all my awkward non-salsa moves, Leah followed me to the community bathroom to make sure I didn't get raped or kidnapped along the way. Afterwards, she put me in a taxi because, as she described it, "at that point, you were just kind of a mess in general."

Wonderful.

That must have been when I blog-diaried from the toilet. My life has officially reached new lows. I've recovered my purse and partial information from last night but now feel even worse about self, alcohol abuse, and certain financial doom.

On the positive, Leah has invited me out to breakfast and has also offered to help search for my missing un-engagement ring. Perhaps she's not an evil bitch after all. I may ask for beauty/life pointers during breakfast.

I hope she picks up the tab.

Comment from Anna P: Website visitors don't come easy these days. It's tough and takes a long time. In many cases, too much time... So much that you might be ready to give up. One of my readers shared a *web traffic service with me and I thought I would share it with you. I was skeptical at first but tried their free trial and it turns out they are able to get dozens of visitors to your website every day! My advertising revenue has increased twentyfold. Check them out here: <scary web link>.*

Date: Monday
Time: Brunch time
Location: Joe's Diner (best breakfast place ever!).
Day Rating (So Far): Two stars, very confusing.

The excitement over seeing my first ever blog diary comment was crushed by the realization that my first ever blog diary comment was sent by a shady Internet solicitor. That scary web link is surely an invitation for a computer virus to invade my iPad, steal my identity, and ruin my life worse than it already is. And I can't even figure out how to delete it. Stupid iPad.

Meanwhile, my breakfast with Leah was satisfying appetite-wise but rather crushing psychologically. I discovered that Leah was an incredibly put together island goddess with wonderful hair, perfect skin, great accessories, and an amazing job where she is her own boss. In addition, she had a sexy boyfriend and an expensive Chanel handbag. So basically she has the best life ever and I have the worst life ever. I hate her. Have I said that yet? I do. Hate her. A lot. But, at the same time, I'm a little confused by her quality personality and seemingly sincere interest in me as a person.

"Are you staying in that huge villa by yourself?" Leah asked after we ordered coffee, eggs, bacon, and a mound of cheesy potatoes.

I tried not to notice her perfectly painted fingernails and the elegant way she sipped from her coffee mug. But I did notice.

"Unfortunately yes," I said, attempting to sip elegantly from my coffee mug and scalding my lip.

"Why?"

Between shovels of eggs and potatoes, I ended up telling Leah practically everything about my entire life. Focusing, obviously, on the happenings of the last twenty-four hours.

"Wow," she said when I was done. "Un-honeymoon. I love it."

My face must have crumpled in on itself because she quickly added, "I mean, that's horrible. I'm so sorry."

"There are worse things," I said, feeling sad and horrendously unattractive.

"Have you any idea where Colin is now?"

(I've noticed that Leah speaks in a unique, highly elegant way as if trained by spendy European tutors while living in mansions and enjoying afternoon tea and learning fancy foreign phrases like *je nes...*whatever. Note to future self: lose awful Midwestern accent and learn to speak in elegant way, as if trained by spendy European tutors.)

"No," I said, deciding not to tell her about Colin's muse-ical artist's loft. "None at all. I've called him a thousand times and – what?"

Leah grimaced over her coffee mug. "Er –" she said slowly. "Well, in some cases you may be better suited to playing hard to get. You know. Pretend he no longer exists, ignore his phone calls, make him win you back. That sort of thing."

"How can I make him win me back when he's the one who dumped me in the first place?"

"Um – well, I guess I don't know."

Obviously, Leah has never been dumped or lied to in her entire life. Who would ever want to dump her or lie to her in the first place? She was highly successful and highly gorgeous with a great personality and super huge boobs.

"In any case," Leah was saying. "The point is that it's time to move on. Forget about Colin and enjoy your un-honeymoon. Go to the beach, go shopping, see the sights. Have some fun." She lifted her coffee mug like it was an exclamation point.

"Nothing better than a solo tropical island vacation," I muttered into my pile of bacon.

"That's where you're wrong," Leah said. "Now you know me."

She smiled, leaning back in her chair and crossing her arms elegantly. She was wearing a long, colorful islandy dress and strappy flat sandals combo I could never pull off due to my height deficiency and general lack of attractiveness. She belonged on the cover of Vogue magazine, not sitting in Joe's Diner with a six (five).

I hate her.

I must have pasted a dubious look on my face because Leah laughed and said, "Come on, Sam. Seriously. I'm trying to be friends here, you know. I like you. You're...funny and...well, I don't get the pleasure of taking care of drunken tourists nearly as often as I'd like."

"Ha," I muttered. "Thanks, I guess. For the funny comment. Not the other one."

(Did you notice that? She called me Sam. Not *Sammy*. Funny how such a small thing can make me feel way more grown up and a lot less dumb and awkward than usual. Sam sounds way cooler and mission-capable than *Sammy*. Sam. Sam Stone. Special Agent Samantha Stone. Ha.)

Leah was watching me, coffee cup raised to her lips. "You're on vacation, Sam," she said over the rim. "It's time to loosen up a little bit."

She grinned, shimmying her shoulders. Half the restaurant turned to drool over her exotic sexiness and huge jiggly boobs. I looked down at my own smallish, non-jiggly boobs and sighed. There was a bacon grease stain on the front of my dress. It was shaped like California. I tried to blot it with my napkin. It didn't work.

"I know the best restaurants, the best beaches," Leah was saying, oblivious to the customers drooling all over her generous bosom. "I own a spa, you know. Free treatments..." She eyed my bacon grease spot warily.

"Fine, fine, okay." I managed a half-hearted laugh. "Friends." (Friends*ish*, at least.)

"Friends." Leah smiled. "Fabulous."

Then I remembered why she looked so familiar to me. She was the female half of the arguing couple I'd seen after getting off the ferry.

"Hey," I said, giving up on my bacon grease stain, which had spread across the entire front of my dress. "I saw you yesterday, just off the ferry dock. With Jimmy."

Leah frowned, then shook her head. "I don't think so," she said.

"Yeah," I said. "Near the Beached Bar. Around...threeish?"

She shook her head again. "I was working," she said. "Definitely wasn't me."

Huh. It definitely *was* her. Why would she lie about that? Maybe she was embarrassed about the arguing?

"So..." Leah changed the subject, eyeing me cautiously.

"What? What is it?"

"Well...now that we're friends and all, might I suggest a new choice in purse wear?"

"What's wrong with my purse?" I looked at the bag, plopped unceremoniously atop our breakfast table. Sure, it was still soggy from getting caught in the rain. And sure, I'd had it for a few years and had repaired the strap a few times. With duct tape. Sure, it had a few stains on it from who knows what. But it wasn't too bad, was it?

"Well..." Leah grimaced, poking at the duct tape with an elegantly sculpted fingernail. "I mean, flesh colors are great and all...for stockings, you know. Not purses. Or clothing. Or...anything besides stockings. Where did you get it anyway? Walmart? And, seriously, what's with the duct tape? It sort of looks like a...hobo bag."

"What's wrong with..." I looked at Leah's purse, an apple green quilted Chanel handbag that probably cost more than I made in a month.

"Do you have any other ones?" she asked.

"Other what? Purses? No. Why would I need more than one purse?"

Leah stared at me, wide eyed. "Seriously?" she said. Then – "where did you say you're from again?"

"Elkton," I said. "It's a small town in –"

"Elkton?" She raised her eyebrows and scrunched up her nose. "How many people live there?"

"1,397, including me."

"What sort of shops do you have?"

"Shops?" I thought for a second. "Well, let's see. There's the Fleet Farm, the Walmart..." I trailed off.

"That's it?" She looked like she'd just learned I had terminal brain cancer and had only six hours to live. "Have you ever been to, like...J Crew? H&M?"

"H&M?" I gasped. "Isn't that...?"

Leah frowned.

"Isn't that, like...a sex place?"

"What? No!" Leah threw her head back and laughed. "That's *S&M*. And it's not a sex place. It's a..." Her voice dropped. "You're not a virgin, are you?"

"No!" I said, slightly offended. Just because I was from a small town and didn't know H&M from S&M didn't automatically mean I was a super old virgin. "I've had sex," I muttered. "I've done...sex things."

"Are you sure?"

"Am I sure I'm not a virgin?" I glared at her. "Yeah, I'm pretty sure I'm not a virgin, Leah."

"Good," she said. "I would have been surprised, but you never know these days."

"Why would you have been surprised?"

"Because of your body," she shrugged.

"My body?" My short, undersized body?

"Yeah," she said. "I'm not, like, into women or anything, so don't get weird when I say this, but you have a super hot bod."

"Yeah, I'm like five feet tall."

"And?"

I didn't say anything. Wasn't that enough?

"But you have all those gorgeous curves!" she said. "Aren't guys after you, like, all the time?"

"No," I said. "Not at all." I thought of Shane and all the flirting. Then Jimmy and all the flirting. Did they look right past the state of my hair and face and see only my short body and all the curves I apparently had but never knew I did? That would be great!

"But...what about this?" I pointed at my forehead. "And this?" I pointed at the bacon grease stain. "And this?" I lifted a strand of thin, dirty blonde hair.

"Stop it," Leah said. "Those things are fixable. You really need to stop with the whole self-deprecation thing. It's annoying."

I shrugged.

"I know!" Her eyes twinkled mischievously. "I have the *best* idea."

"What?" I sat forward in my chair. "What is it?" I *loved* best ideas, even more than regular ones! I really hoped it wasn't a sex thing.

"*We* are gonna go shopping."

My heart sank. I was hoping for something less...spendy.

"We're going to have a whole day of shopping," Leah rambled on excitedly. "We can get you a new purse. A way better purse. And some new clothes. Clothes that accentuate all those curves. We'll start in Cruz Bay, see what we find, and then we'll pop on over to St. Thomas. Ooh, this is going to be so great!"

She seemed so excited about all the shopping, I didn't have the heart to tell her that I was too poor to even pay for breakfast. Oh *God*, how I wished I was a tall, gorgeous rich person instead of a short, average looking poor person.

Leah was squinting, studying my face. "You know," she said. "Maybe, if you want to, perhaps consider having a facial. My treat. I mean, only if you want to. But you definitely should. Tighten up the pores, even out the tone."

Tone? Pores? What?

"A facial?" I said. "Um..." My heart sank.

(Confession: So I don't exactly know what a facial is. I mean, it's not like spas and facials just happen in Elkton, so it's not technically my fault. It's like a face mask, right?)

"And a blowout," she continued, assessing the negative state of my hair and face, squinting from time to time and generally making me feel like a horribly unattractive science experiment gone awry.

"A blowout?" That didn't sound good. That was *definitely* a sex thing.

Leah sat up, jostling her boobs again. The restaurant-goers collectively paused what they were doing to watch.

"And your eyebrows need threading, and maybe some highlights around your face," she said. "And bangs, definitely bangs. I mean, your forehead, Jesus Christ. Your whole body needs exfoliation. And your nails. Please stop biting them. Like now. And, like I said, some major shopping. Extensions! Oh my God – a total makeover. This is gonna be –"

"Whoa. Hang on a second." My cheeks felt hot. "Are you serious?"

My eyes went swimmy. My bacon turned to a hard pit of vomitousness in my belly. Leah looked like an exotic Jessica Alba while I looked like a long-haired girl version of Clay Aiken. It wasn't fair. Nothing was fair. Like it's my fault Elkton has only one stylist – an eighty-six year old, half-blind, trembly fingered woman named Vera. She gives everyone the same exact haircut, but we pretend not to notice because she's so old and sad looking and lives alone and is very, very old.

Now I felt like I was stuck in a bad after school special where the lovely girl tries to befriend the sad ugly girl and make her into a better overall person and all it does is cause the sad ugly girl to hate herself and commit suicide.

After my initial surge of horror passed, I started feeling sort of conflicted and partially intrigued. This spa-owning, Chanel handbag toting, gorgeous beach goddess was offering me my very own un-honeymoon tropical island makeover. For free. I'd go back to Elkton all glowy and amazing with bangs and a new personality. I'd confront my stupid un-friends and shake my new bangs and highlights all over them. I'd tell Kelly I quit, pack my bags, and move to Minneapolis. Start over. New job, new friends, new life. Hmmm...

"So...no makeover?" Leah stared at me, looking confused.

"No, I meant..." I sighed.

What did I mean? Who was I kidding, thinking I'd ever actually do something like leave Elkton and move to the big city? No one leaves Elkton. Not my family, not my friends, not me. Ever. What was the point in even pretending? I would live in Elkton until I died, like Vera, alone in my tiny house waiting for visitors who never came and asking the neighbor children to shovel my driveway and help me walk across the road. I had a lot to look forward to. Blah.

"Are you okay, Sam?"

"I'm fine."

I am not fine. I am a wretched, disgusting mess of a human being who gets curses put on her and gets dumped at the altar on her wedding day. I want nothing more than to embody confidence, courage, determination, and lots of other positive feminist qualities, but instead I feel completely horrible about my physical appearance and shitty attitude. I'm certain that the wedding day dumpage, missing ring, drunken un-salsa dancing, and new spa-owning friend telling me I need a makeover are all byproducts of feeling dumb and ugly most of the time. I mean all of the time. My life has become positively unbearable; I want to crawl under my breakfast chair and die.

"Did I get carried away?" Leah was saying. Her face went red again. "I'm sorry, I always do that. I'm so sorry." She sighed. "Are you okay? Sam?"

To my horror, I burst into tears in front of her and the entire diner. "You think everything about me sucks!" I sob yelled. "My hair, my face, my eyebrows, my forehead, my choice in purse wear, my...face." I'd already forgotten all about her self-deprecation comment of earlier.

"Oh Sam, I didn't mean...Shoot, I always do this." Leah sighed, handing me a napkin to cry into. I cried into it, loudly.

"You don't need a makeover, Sam. It's not your fault that you look like...Clay Aiken." Her voice dropped to a whisper, like talking about Clay Aiken would cause him to materialize next to her and burst into song. "It really isn't your fault," she said. "I just got excited because, well, I don't have a lot of girlfriends, and I thought it would be fun. You know, you're on vacation. You could go home with a sexy new look or something." She sighed, rubbing her cheek. "This always worked for Oprah. I'm so sorry. Forget I said anything."

I think Leah felt genuinely bad, despite being so horrible and evil and great looking. Her eyes had gone swimmy and she actually seemed very embarrassed. But she still looked awesome, so I continued to hate her.

"I'm so sorry Sam," she said again. "You're great just the way you are. Seriously forget I said anything. Forget the whole thing. No makeover. Just beaches, shopping, and cocktails, okay?"

"Oh no," I said, wiping snot off my hands and face. "I definitely want the free makeover. I mean...if it's still free."

Leah looked stunned. Then she burst out laughing. "You do want the makeover?" she said. "Thank God."

"It's mainly the haircut though, right? That makes me look like...like Clay Aiken?" I sounded sad and desperate.

"Wouldn't you say that it's mainly the haircut?" (Please, please say it's the haircut.)

Leah stared at me warily. "Let's just see, shall we?"

Gorgeous spa-owning bitch.

Time: After brunch time
Location: Beached Bar

After breakfast, which Leah paid for, we went back to the Beached Bar to pick up Leah's car, retrace my steps from the night before, and hopefully uncover my missing un-engagement ring in record time. Leah's Jeep Wrangler was white with hand painted orchids on the sides. It was the most elegant Jeep design I'd ever seen. I wanted it desperately. I thought of the 1998 teal Dodge Neon rust bucket with 197,000 miles and no heater or radio waiting for me back home. Stupid.

Once at the bar, I crawled around on my hands and knees for an eon, unsuccessfully locating my lost ring/future mortgage payments. I even mustered up the courage to approach the middle-aged morning bartendress – a pear-shaped, washed-up bleached blonde who'd spent way too much time in the sun during her younger years. Her skin looked like a combination of wrinkles, saran wrap, and used tissue paper. Unfortunately for me, the morning bartendress knew nothing about anything and was generally very unhelpful and scowly.

Thinking of my toilet blog, I tried to drag Leah into the community bathroom to search for the ring. She waited outside while I bandaged my hands with paper towels and poked around the toilet for awhile. I found only toilet paper and a nasty used condom. It was the most disgusting thing I'd ever had to do. But, as a proper 007 would say, it must have been done. I mean, it must be done. Or whatever.

After un-bandaging my hands and washing them 1,000+ times, I popped back over to the bar with Leah for a quick morning cocktail.

"It's Monday," I realized after ordering an extra spicy Bloody Mary from the scowly, poor-skinned bartendress.

"Yeah?" Leah said, ordering a mimosa.

"You don't have to work on Mondays?"

"The spa is closed on Mondays," Leah said. "We're only open on the weekends."

"You only work on the weekends?"

"Well, I do some stuff during the week, too. Office stuff. Paperwork, mostly. But, yeah, mainly only on the weekends."

That made sense. Leah was a gorgeous bitch with the job that only required work on the weekends. Personally, I would love to have a job that only required work on the weekends and paid me enough to carry designer handbags and wear thousand dollar outfits. I'd have the entire week to sleep in and catch up on *America's Next Top Model* episodes and work on looking chic and amazing. She was probably super rich with old family money and a trust fund and has the spa for a hobby, not as an actual job. Fucking lame. I mean, great for her.

"So you just came to St. John for a visit and never went back to Virginia?" I asked jealously. "Then you opened a spa and only work on weekends?" How foolish and romantic and wonderfully amazing. She was probably super rich with old family money and a trust fund and has the spa for a hobby, not as an actual job. Fucking lame. I mean, great for her.

"What about your family?" I asked after Leah didn't respond. "Don't you miss them?"

Leah frowned into her drink. "My parents died when I was 14," she said. "They were both only children."

"Oh," I said. "I'm sorry."

She shrugged. "It's okay," she said. "I still have my grandfather. We're very close."

"Any siblings?"

Leah scowled, her eyes going dark. Right. I decided to change the subject. No family talk. Got it.

"So, how long have you and Jimmy been together?"

She sighed. "Oh, let's see. About...almost a year, now. He moved here last winter."

"How did you guys meet?"

"He came into the spa," she smiled. "With a bouquet of bougainvillea. Flowers of my home...state." She glanced at me. Then sighed. "It was so romantic."

I snorted despite myself. "Sorry," I said. Leah rolled her eyes.

"What about the taxi?" Leah asked, shifting the subject back to the ring. "Have you called them and asked if they've seen your ring? Though I doubt they'd even report a diamond if they found one."

I shook my head. "I already called them. And it's a garnet, not a diamond."

"A what?"

"A garnet. Like a...gemstone. Not a diamond."

Leah frowned.

"I know, right? Who gets a non-diamond engagement ring?" I shrugged, tears pricking my eyes. "I thought it was special."

"It is special," said Leah. "I mean, it was special...to you."

"I guess," I said. "Until I found out that Colin just got it at some dumb jewelry store."

"What jewelry store?"

I dug the magazine ad out of my purse and unfolded it. "Sapphire Junction," I said. "On St. Thomas."

"What is this?" Leah reached for the ad.

"My ring," I said. "I came across it in a magazine ad on the way down here."

Leah's face went white. "But..."

"But what?" I said.

"I thought..." Leah shook her head. "So Colin gave you this ring," she pointed to the ad. "And said he designed it himself? When he proposed to you?"

I nodded. "He said he designed it, but he did not. Obviously." I took a sip of my Bloody. "Stupid asshole," I muttered. The scowly bartendress glanced up at me. "Not you," I said. She rolled her eyes.

"It's so beautiful," Leah whispered, staring at the ad.

I snorted again. "Yeah, if you like that kind of thing. Dime a dozen, apparently."

Leah looked at me, her eyes dark and wide. "What?"

"Dime a dozen? It's an expression, you know. It means...commonplace. Not one-of-a-kind, specially designed just for..." I trailed off. "Wait – didn't you say that I didn't have the ring on when I got into the taxi last night?" (I distinctly remember her saying this because, after she mentioned it at breakfast, I thought it might be nice to have a proper notebook to take down evidence-tracking notes about the missing ring and other things.)

Leah nodded, distracted. "Uh huh."

"Then why would you tell me to call them?"

"Um…" She didn't look up from the ad. "I thought you already called them," she said.

"I did, but… Leah?"

"Hmm? Yes, I just…why is it torn in half?"

I plucked the ad from her fingers and put it back in my purse. "It's a long story. I got startled while ripping it out."

She looked at me quizzically.

"Er – I guess that's basically the whole story." I trailed off again. "You don't look so great," I said. "Are you okay? Leah?"

Leah watched me zip my purse, the color slowly returning to her face. "Have you showed that ad to anyone?" she asked.

"No," I said. "I just ripped it out of the magazine so I could stare at it and feel bad about myself later, probably while eating an entire box of Oreos and watching my *Love Actually* DVD. But I was actually thinking about making some copies and hanging them up on some telephone poles and community boards and stuff. Wait – does St. John even have telephone poles and community boards? How about a copier?"

Leah didn't answer.

"Are you sure you're okay?" She was starting to look pretty sick. But still awesome, obviously.

"Actually, I'm not feeling so well," she said. "I think I'm going to go lie down."

She quickly gathered her things and pressed her lips together like she was trying desperately not to barf.

"Let's meet up for dinner, okay? There's a great little spot just up the road. It's called Nona's Place. Red sign. You can't miss it. Seven o'clock, okay? Meet me there. Don't be late."

She got up and tucked her clutch under her arm. "And Sam?" she said. "Be careful who you show that picture to, okay?"

"Why?"

"Just trust me. And no copies. No community boards. Okay?"

Then she walked away, all elegant and dumb, hips sashaying, mahogany hair swinging all over the place.

People like me get sick and barf all over everything. People like Leah get sick and they go take a nap and make dinner plans and sashay around the island while swinging their shiny hair from side to side.

Stupid.

In any event, I'm signing off now so I can continue the search for my missing ring while feeling mediumly bad about my life and wedding-day dumpage but a little excited about my probable free makeover.

Also, I guess I'm back to just one potential island sex fling since Jimmy the hottie bartender is dating a perfect ten model. But Shane is nowhere to be found and I have no way of reaching him because I don't have his phone number or his island address. This is probably a good thing.

Back to square one – broke, single, unfortunate looking, and totally, completely alone.

Sigh.

Date: Monday
Time: Mid-afternoonish
Location: Cruz Bay beach.
Day Rating (So Far): Medium.

After Leah left to nap off her impromptu sickness, I wandered aimlessly down the curvy gorgeous roads of St. John. Like a leaf on the wind. Like a cloud in the sky. And so on.

I took this boring alone time as an opportunity to ponder my life's events over the past three days. Namely (1) leaving Elkton for the first time ever (except for a week-long bible camp in Wisconsin when I was eight, where I was sent home after the second day because I wouldn't stop crying and couldn't participate in the Jesus-praising songs because of all the crying), and (2) traveling cross-country to stay alone on a romantic tropical island and finding myself in a mystery web of lost-ring intrigue.

It was all starting to seem very exciting and romantic, and I congratulated myself for living such an exciting and romantic life and for making it so far into the day without any Xanax.

After drifting around like a...like a...piece of drift-wood...for quite some time, thinking and working on my base tan and burning off my breakfast calories and Bloody Mary beverage, I eventually found myself outside a flesh-colored building that looked a bit like a police station due to the number of police cars and police bikes parked in the parking lot. (And the sign that said 'Island Police Building' on the front.) I figured it wouldn't hurt to meander in and see if I could file a lost-ring report or whatever they do for lost goods on foreign tropical islands. (I would also like to know who chooses flesh colored paint and thinks it's going to look good on anything. FYI – it doesn't. I learned this from Leah. See, I'm learning so much already!)

After walking into the police station, the lady at the front desk spoke very harshly toward me and basically made me feel both incapable and highly stupid. I explained to her a few times that I'd experienced a significant property loss and needed to report it to someone of authority. She finally rolled her eyes and pointed to a plastic police bench.

I sat on the plastic police bench for what felt like days before a very tall, very dark, very skinny islander policeman in his late fifties came to get me. He was dressed to the nines in crisp, spotless white and made me feel very uncomfortable and sweaty in my skimpy black sundress with largish bacon grease stain, ugly purse, and duct-taped vacation flip flops.

As the ridiculously tall policeman led me toward his desk, I suddenly realized that visiting the Police Building was the worst idea I've ever had. Even worse than going on my stupid honeymoon by myself. But since I was already there, I felt very over-committed and nervous. I briefly thought about making a run for it but was unsure as to what happens to tourists who run from foreign police stations. I was too afraid of winding up in that scary hungry-lesbian prison to find out.

Policeman Officer Calvin Gregory sat me down at his perfectly organized desk with his perfectly sharpened pencils and fresh paged notebooks and asked me what was wrong. I was so sweaty and panicky and put off by his super organizing skills that I momentarily whack attacked and settled into a long series of short, wheezy coughs. By the time I finished, my head and throat were on fire. I swallowed repeatedly, eventually managing to tell him through a series of coughs and stutters that I'd lost my ring the night before.

"When did you notice the ring was missing?"

Policeman Gregory's accent turned 'the' to 'da' and was generally very charming and wonderful.

"When I woke up this morning." (Good. Solid. Succinct and to the point. Great answer.)

"And the last time you remember seeing it?"

Hmm...that was tricky. I definitely remember having it when I got to the bar, because Jimmy was staring at it, making me wish I'd left it at home or at the villa or anywhere besides my finger. Then Shane showed up. Then the Cherry Bombs happened.

"I had it on when I got to the bar last night," I said finally. "I remember glancing at it when I ordered my first drink because the bartender, er – never mind."

Officer Gregory sat as still as a statue. Watching me. Judging me. I started sweating again.

"Um – I don't really remember seeing it after that though," I stuttered. "It was just...gone. Which is totally weird. I mean, that ring was so tight on my finger, I never took it off. Ever. That's the whole reason I forgot to leave it at home. I just never even noticed it because it was always there. It was sized too small, you know, because my fiancé, I mean, ex-fiancé, er – never mind. In any case, it was hard to get off. Like really, really hard. Crisco and elbow grease, that's what I always used to say."

I was rambling like a mad person, sounding completely insane and slightly unbalanced. It was a horrible turn of events, but I couldn't stop myself.

"I would have had to take it off," I explained. "That's what I'm trying to say, I guess. It never would have just slipped off. But I never would have taken it off either. It's a five thousand dollar ring. I mean..." I trailed off.

Suddenly, it hit me.

"Maybe I *didn't* lose the ring," I said. "Maybe it was stolen!"

(Gasp. Pause for effect.)

Ta da! Thank you, ladies and gentlemen, thank you. Pint-sized Sammy Stone from Armpit-town, Minnesota figured out everything! The ring was stolen, not lost. I'd file a police report and let the cops do their jobs. The ring would be recovered before the end of my un-honeymoon and everything would be the way it was supposed to be! Hurrah!

Huge sigh of relief.

Or not.

"Let me get this straight," Officer G. said, steepling his fingers in that common asshole gesture that all assholes do. "You wore a five thousand dollar engagement ring to the Beached Bar last night. You proceeded to get extremely intoxicated," he paused. I didn't argue. He continued.

"A friend put you in a cab and, when you woke up this morning, the ring was gone. Now you believe the ring that you yourself can barely pry off your finger was stolen. Right off your finger?"

"Yes," I said meekly. It didn't sound so great when he said it like that.

"Is the ring insured?"

"Um, er – well, I think so. I'm not sure, I guess. There was some paperwork...I think..."

(Did I ever fill out that paperwork? I don't think so. Crap. Note to future self: get way better at actually filling out important paperwork. Was there even paperwork? I'm so confused.)

Officer G. grabbed a notebook and a perfectly sharpened pencil. "Can you describe it for me?"

"The ring?" I asked, like a total idiot. Of course he meant the ring! Duh! I shook my head, knowing I would feel like a total idiot for the rest of the conversation. Even more so than I already did.

I unzipped my purse, taking out the half ad I'd torn from the airplane magazine. My fingers were so shaky with policeman fright that the ad slipped out of my hand and fell to the ground. To make matters worse, when I bent down to pick up the ad, I smashed my forehead against the edge of the desk with a loud, distinct thud. I may or may not have actually shifted the desk, also.

Feelings of awful inadequacy washed over me. I wished I'd taken a dozen Xanax prior to visiting the police station. I wished I'd never stepped foot into the police station in the first place. I wished I could just crawl under Officer G's perfectly organized police desk and die.

Swallowing my embarrassment, I returned upright to hand the ad to Officer G. We both ignored the throbbing red spot on my forehead and my overly-swimmy eyes.

Officer G. unfolded the ad. He glared at me.

"What is this?" It came out "What eez 'dis?"

He sounded mean or angry, put together. Was it illegal to tear an ad out of a magazine in a foreign country? Crap. That would be just my luck. Handing proof of an illegal activity directly to a policeman. Great job, Sammy.

"Well, you see –" I was sweating so bad. My head was on fire, my scalp was sweating, even my groinal area was sweating. Everything was gross and sweating. I worried about my adrenals. I vowed to learn everything I could about curses so I could put a curse on stupid Lena Olofsson as soon as possible and see how she liked it.

"I…I…was on the plane to St. Thomas, and I came across this in a magazine." My voice sounded super high and weird. "It's the exact same ring as the one I have – or had. So I took it, the ad… I'm not sure why." *Love Actually! Oreos!*

I sunk an inch lower in my chair, head throbbing. I wanted to disappear. I had once again executed on a horrible idea and felt more stupid than ever.

(Note to future self: stop following through on horrible ideas such as going on un-honeymoon alone and prancing around in police station with an illegally ripped out magazine ad.)

"Is this a joke?" Officer G. asked, his eyes hard.

"What?" I asked, confused. "No! No… it looks exactly like

that, I swear."

Officer G. excused himself. I watched him out of the corner of my eye as he strode across the station toward another policeman. The two of them huddled their heads together and whispered angrily back and forth for quite some time.

I sat there staring at them, wondering what I'd gotten myself into. I considered running away again but knew I lacked both speed and confidence. Plus, I wanted my ad back so I could have it to clutch and sob over during *Love Actually*.

The policeman with whom Officer G. was conversing was a short, super thick and muscly islander with a shaved head and a sparkly pinky ring. I'd never seen a man with a pinky ring before and definitely could have done without it. Didn't he know that pinky rings went out of style in the 1970s? Should I tell him?

I didn't know what to do with myself while the evil police dudes were talking, so I ended up just sitting there, picking at my cuticles and unsuccessfully trying to overhear what they were saying. They took turns glancing at me and glaring. My face got even hotter. My entire head felt like it was about to explode.

I eventually dug my cell phone out of my purse and pretend-checked my messages, hoping it would help with my almost-exploding head situation. While doing my pretend-checking, I saw that my dick boss, Kelly (a guy), tried calling me several times and even had the nerve to send a follow up text asking me to call him! I stewed. Who calls someone on their un-honeymoon and demands an immediate response via text message? I'll tell you who: assholes. Assholes do that. I'd wager a bet that the reason for Kelly's call was neither important nor urgent. I would rather crawl under the police desk and die than ever hear Kelly's voice again. I decided that (1) I would absolutely *not* respond since I am on my un-honeymoon, which Kelly is fully aware of and (2) I hated Kelly so much I wanted to shoot him in the face and then step on him. Put together!

"May I see your passport?" Officer G. was back with the ad, startling me. I dropped my cell phone. Luckily the phone landed in my lap and not on the floor.

"Huh?" I managed. My forehead throbbed.

"Your passport. May I see it please?"

I took the ad back from him and stuffed it in my purse. "I

don't have it with me. It's back at my villa."

"Name please."

"Er – Sam...my?"

"Full name please."

I started sweating again. "Sammy Stone. Sam. Samantha Lynn Stone, I mean."

"Where is your villa?"

Christ. What was this? One thousand question day? All I wanted to do was file a police report and move on with my life.

"Um, at the top of the hill. Of the ladder. Jacob's Ladder, or whatever. It's called Blissful Villa."

"You have been here before, yes?"

"No," I said. "This is my first time. Ever. I mean, I've never even been on an airplane before. Except for yesterday. It wasn't great, to be honest."

"Your first time here?" Officer G. repeated. "To St. John?"

"St. John, St. Thomas...all of the above," I said. "I've only ever been to Minnesota and Wisconsin. But, you know, this place is...okay. So far. It's very hot."

"How long are you planning to stay?" Officer G. said, eyeing me warily.

"Er – um, Saturday. I leave on Saturday."

"Saturday. Fine." He gestured for me to stand up and follow him. I did, wondering if he was going to lead me to the area where I could fill out some paperwork about my stolen/missing ring. Instead, he led me to the front door.

"Goodbye," he said abruptly.

But the police report! The criminal investigation! The successful recovery and return of my ring before I went back home! I figured there would be questions, evidence taking, suspect lists, and more police things to do. At least.

"But my ring," I stammered as Officer G. pushed me out the door.

"I am sorry," he said, his wiry frame half-blocking the doorway. "I do not find your visit very humorous, nor does my partner. We cannot help you. Please do not come back."

Before I knew what was happening, I was back on the scalding streets of Cruz Bay.

"What the hell?" I muttered to myself. I made a mental note

to ask Leah if she knew of anyone who specialized in curse-breaking. Then I popped a whole Xanax, just to make it through the situation in one piece.

My walk back to the beach was filled with jumbled thoughts of shoddy police work and alcohol-induced memory loss. I sort of figured, at this point, that there may be much more to my lost un-engagement ring than initially met the eye. Why was everyone so weird about it? First Leah, then Officer Gregory. It was weird, right?

I decided to go on a mission to find a bona fide sleuthing notebook in which to take down notes on suspects and other evidence. If the police wouldn't help me find my ring, I'd have to go ahead and do it myself. I needed that ring or I'd lose my dumb townhouse. And everyone already knows what would happen to me if I lost my dumb townhouse.

Walking down the boardwalk, I popped into the first tourist shop I saw. I just so happened to find a lovely leather bound skinny lined journal book just sitting there waiting for me to buy and use it. Unfortunately, I was forced to use my nearly maxed out credit card for the $19.79 investment. Plus tax. I left the shop feeling generally horrible and financially insecure but definitely excited about my new notebook purchase. Sure, I could have used my iPad, but what's the fun in that? Like 007 ever uses an iPad for note taking. I'm sure he has his own specialized notebook in which to jot down notes and clues and things, just like me. Besides, I wasn't too sure about the whole sand in the wireless keyboard thing. I mean, the iPad and its keyboard companion were like the most expensive things I'd ever owned. I really didn't want to ruin them so soon.

I brought my new notebook to the beach and plopped down in the sizzling white sand to work on my suspect/evidence list while simultaneously evolving my base tan. I prided myself on such successful multi-tasking and mission-accomplishing and, after pondering my recent life events, I spent a solid hour compiling a ring stealing suspect list, scenario situations, and evidence.

Possible Scenario Situations:

- Ring was lost
- Ring was stolen
- Ring was lost and then stolen

Suspect List:
- René the crappy caretaker
- Shane
- Jimmy
- Leah
- Me
- Guy from plane who called me 'cowgirl' and breathed into my hair and ear (not likely)
- Unknown/Other

Evidence and/or Facts
- Ring was stolen/lost *after* getting to the bar and flirting with Jimmy, the sexy green-eyed bartender.
- Ring was stolen/lost *before* waking up in my sweaty villa the next morning.
- Leah *says* she didn't see the ring before putting me into the taxi, but the evidence is uncertain.
- Leah had a very strange reaction to the ad.
- Policeman had a very strange reaction to the ad.
- Beached Bar bartendress has not seen the ring. This means nothing as she was not working last night.

Next steps:
- Search Jeep just in case ring flew off finger unnoticed at some point while driving.
- Return to Beached Bar when Jimmy's shift starts and ask if he knows anything. Try not to flirt with him despite his total hotness and flirty smiles.
- Go to Sapphire Junction crap non-diamond jewelry shop and ask around about the ring and search for clues, though if I see a duplicate of my un-engagement ring, I just might die.
- Figure out the location of the muse-ical artist's loft and track down assholio ex-fiancé. Mentally judo him for being a disgusting pig, liar, and total asshole. This has nothing to do with anything, except to support my ability to heal and move on

emotionally.

- Determine the status of ring insurance paperwork, as a largish insurance pay out would be a wonderful remedy for my current financial crisis.

I closed the notebook and stared out over the ocean for a bit, congratulating myself for such adequate and successful mission work. I was definitely off to a great start, for a junior sleuth, anyway.

It was a little exiting, you know. Having a ring-finding mission. I mean, the possibility of having both a mysterious adventure and an actual island hobby was the most exciting thing that has happened to me since...well...ever. Losing a ring and recovering it on my own through super-successful sleuthing methodologies? Balls! I would return to Elkton with my head held high and a very exciting un-honeymoon story to share with all my loser un-friends.

I tried not to think about the possibility that my ring may or may not already be en route to Japan, Moscow, or some other faraway place. Or at the bottom of the vast ocean, currently being eaten by sea creature.

I have decided to focus on the positive and, also, I have nothing better to do besides return to my sweaty villa and read my boring historical travel novel.

Date: Monday
Time: Mid-afternoonish
Location: Water Tide Restaurant.
Day Rating (So Far): Five glorious stars.

So many wonderful things have happened in the last hour, I don't even know where to start! I feel very on top of the world despite my current lack of makeover and ring-locating failures. I've even started to wonder if perhaps my curse has finally broken. (But, I don't want to get my hopes up in case the curse is not actually broken.)

After finishing my first ever detective journal entry, I searched my Jeep inside and out, finding only an old packet of cheese crackers and an empty beer can. By the time I was done searching, I figured I'd burned about eight thousand calories walking around town and having a heart attack at the police station and journaling and searching my Jeep. I was starving and thirsty and needed a snack and a cocktail in the worst way.

As I meandered down the boardwalk, looking for a place to grab a sit down and a snack, guess who I ran into?

You'll never guess.

I'll give you a hint: sexy, hot, *and* cute all wrapped up into one perfectly chiseled, perfectly dimpled, perfectly tanned cute-butted package.

Yessss! My island sex god has returned again!

It just so happened that I came across Shane while he was on his cell phone muttering something about something "turning up somewhere." When he saw me, he looked like he'd just found a pot of gold at the end of a double rainbow. It made me feel very confident and good looking, despite still being the "before" photo of the before-and-after makeover situation. I figured it was all those curves Leah told me I had. I wished I'd known about those earlier.

Anyway, I'm currently waiting at the lunch table for Shane to finish his longish cellular phone conversation so we can have a snack. And a cocktail.

On the super plus side, my romantic island lover paused his cell phone conversation long enough to offer to take me on a Jeep tour of St. John, after which we will surely drink lots of alcohol, make out, and have tons of delicious round-the-clock island sex. Yesss!

I'm signing off to order my cocktail and peruse the snack menu. My face has started feeling a bit crispy from the island sun, so I should probably at least try to apply sunscreen at some point in the near future. And follow up with Leah on the timing of my free makeover. I may decide to go on a semi-permanent blog hiatus until post-sexual marathon recovery but it will depend on my energy levels, of course.

Also, I will plan to resume my ring-detection tactics after all the sexual marathons have ended. Then, I will solve the ring mission, find my ring, and go home with new inner confidence as the gorgeously tanned beach goddess who received a free spa makeover *and* had a romantic fling with an island sex god *and* recovered a stolen ring through accurate sleuthing. Hurrah!

I will return to Elkton looking elegant and confident and stay just long enough to gather my belongings, quit my horrid job, and give all of Elkton the middle finger.

Best. Vacation. Ever.

Date: Monday
Time: 6:30ish p.m.
Location: Sweltering villa, en route to Beached Bar after failed-sexual-marathon-attempt.
Day Rating (So Far): Ugh.

Shane is officially bipolar or suffering from multiple personalities, or both. One minute he loves me and we're making out and lap grinding in the ocean, and I'm thinking it's finally the start of my romantic sexual marathon. The next minute, he's running off with some stupid story about work and bosses and deadlines. And I might have accidentally yelled at him, too.

Recap:
The whole thing started off in an incredibly positive filled-with-potential fashion. After running into Shane on the boardwalk, we convened at Water's Edge restaurant where we split a snack of fish tacos, sipped white wine, and gazed on the ocean like casually wealthy celebrities.

While sipping my wine and eating my fish tacos, I felt highly elegant and upscale. Leah had given me a chic bun hairdo after our breakfast and the most gorgeous island god in the world was still into me despite multiple embarrassing displays of over-drinkage and general awkwardness. It was probably the best moment of my whole life.

After we inhaled the fish tacos and consumed an infinity amount of wine, Shane paid for our snack and went off to grab his Jeep before the credit card came back. I took proper initiative and signed the receipt like bona fide future girlfriend material, adding a generous tip for the server and everything. I tucked the wallet into my purse, ran to the ferry dock, and hopped into Shane's rental Jeep Wrangler, which was a glittery emerald green.

We peeled out of the parking lot like a true romantic island couple, and I'm pretty sure the entire island was envious of my arm candy and wondering how they could get similar arm candy of their own. But they can't! Cuz it's mine!

After a bit of driving around, listening to island tunes, and answering more of Shane's interesting questions about me and my life and everything about me, we stopped at a magical beach overlook and gazed romantically at the gorgeous sights below.

I tried to snap a few couple-selfies with my cell phone to prove my tropical hot guy coupledom, but Shane was acting very camera shy and instead took photos of me gazing romantically at gorgeous sights by myself, like a total loser.

(Note to future self: sneak a photo of Shane so I can gaze at it post-return to gray, dreary Elkton. Then I will always know that meeting him and flirting with him did actually happen and he does actually exist. And he did actually talk to me. I wonder if Shane has photo-phobia or simply doesn't want photos of himself with a six (five). I'm trying not to think about it.)

Once we were done with the magical beach overlook, we drove down the coast to Trunk Bay which, according to Shane, was one of the most photographed beaches on the whole island. When we parked in the parking lot, Shane came around and opened my door for me like a real-life boyfriend would. (I love him.) We proceeded to wander down to the beach while holding hands romantically.

I started rambling on and on about how I'd never seen a beach before and how the ocean was so wonderful and how the colors were so wonderfully intense and how my eyes must have been underdeveloped from living in browns and grays all my life. Shane politely ignored me and checked his phone like a hundred times. He was probably checking for text messages from the non-island girlfriend he was supposed to have broken up with already.

Then, the most wonderful thing happened in all the world.

We got naked.

Well, not quite. But almost. Close enough to count, anyway.

I wanted to do a quick splash in the ocean since I'd not had the opportunity to do so and it was on my tropical island to-do list. Also, ocean water is supposed to be very good for both the hair and the skin. And I definitely needed help in both of those areas.

The beach was deserted, so I did what I never would have done if not on a tropical island un-honeymoon and a little tipsy from a half bottle of wine: I stripped down to my padded push-up bra and sexy polka dot underpants and ran sideways into the water.

(By the way – I am *so* glad I was wearing sexy polka dot underpants and not my dimply-cheek-bearing thong. I figured the sun was so blinding that there was no possible way Shane could see my thigh/butt cheek cellulite, especially since I was running sideways.)

The water was refreshingly cool and felt so incredible I could have died. I splashed around a bit and hoped Shane would hop in after me, but he didn't.

Just so you know, standing alone in the ocean while a sex god stares at you from the shore is pretty much the lamest situation ever, so I splashed about a bit more, floated on my back, and did an ocean handstand that certainly looked casually fun, physically impressive, and technically sound.

"Come in!" I called after my successfully executed handstand. Shane looked so chiseled and lovely on shore, all squinty eyed and attractive. Seeing him made me miss Colin more than I wanted to admit, but I reminded myself to stop thinking about my stupid ex-fiancé and to focus on moving on emotionally while having a short-term sexual fling with a tropical stranger instead.

Shane seemed stressed and uncomfortable, looking around guiltily like he was waiting for his non-island girlfriend to come and kick his ass. But there was no one around but us.

"Come on! Come in!" I hollered.

I would beg if I had to. I would drag him into the ocean myself. It was already the second day of my un-honeymoon, and I was tired of waiting for Shane to initiate all the sexual marathons. The clock was ticking. I decided to stand up for my sexual rights and take the lead. I wasn't about to let my chance at real physical vacation activity pass me by.

Shane stepped closer to the water and waved me to shore. "I don't have my suit on!" he called.

"What?" I dog paddled further away. "Me neither!" I shouted. "Who cares, get out here!"

"I'm not –" he hesitated. "Oh screw it."

He pulled his shirt over his head and dropped it to the sand. When I saw his abs, I nearly had the best orgasm of my life. His body was an Italian statue, all hard-muscled and wonderful. I felt the immediate need to touch his muscles right away. All of them. It was like his abs had magical magnetic powers and my fingers and eyes and lap area were all trapped in his magnetic ab-field, trying unsuccessfully to fight the magnetic powers of his abs.

The world became even more glorious when Shane pulled down his shorts, kicked them onto the sand, and raced into the water. Naked. Completely, 100 percent naked.

(Thank you God. Thank you God. Life has once again become miraculous and filled with amazing sights! I duly vow to protect the mental image of Shane's naked body for the rest of time, dusting it off only when absolutely needed. Or every day, all the time. Oh the hip bone definition. The muscles. The shoulders. The tan lines. The biceps. The penis. His real live penis! I've actually seen it, and it's magnificent!)

Shane swam out to meet me, laughing. "You're crazy," he said, pulling me close. (Hurrah! He was pulling me close!)

I was immediately grateful for the following things: (1) drool-hiding ocean water, (2) close proximity of a gorgeous naked man and his similarly naked penis, and (3) cellulite-hiding ocean water.

Shane slid between my legs, and I wrapped my arms around his neck. We floated in the water, gazing romantically into each others' eyes and water hugging for quite some time. I couldn't stop thinking about his total nakedness, especially his below-water nakedness. I wondered if ocean sex was too slutty to consider. It probably was, with all the sea creatures and things floating around.

"I want to kiss you," he whispered, touching his forehead to mine. Yessss, yessssss!

"Me too," I sighed. "So bad." *Do it*, I thought to myself. Just do it already!

He laughed. "You just say whatever's on your mind, don't you?"

Oh *God*. I must have said that last bit out loud.

"There's just –" He hesitated.

Great. He has a girlfriend. He's married. He's gay.

"What?" I asked, hoping my face looked both sexy and inquisitive. Grateful, once again, for the drool-hiding ocean water.

"Never mind," he said. "It's just…oh, fuck it."

Shane caught my lips and kissed me like he was a highly experienced sex god and I was his sexual slave. My whole body caught fire. I felt Shane's below-water heat and wrapped my legs around his waist, thankful there was a polka-dot panty crotch between us so I didn't have to feel overly slutty and worry about sea creatures floating near places they shouldn't.

Shane was officially a way better kisser than Colin with much nicer lips and much better muscle definition and everything. I was delirious with thoughts of our future marathon sexing and so on.

His hands grabbed my butt, pulling my covered-up naughty bits against his naked naughty bits, and we proceeded to lap grind with each other for quite a bit of time. I would have gladly spent the entire rest of my life growing pruny in the ocean with Shane between my thighs, and I never, ever, ever wanted the moment to end. Ever.

But, of course, it did.

"Look Dad! Sexy in the water!"

Shane and I broke away from each other instantly, feeling guilty (Shane) and pissed/slutty (me).

A random asshole kid in crotch-hugging swim trunks was standing on the shore pointing at us. A large scary adult stood next to him, giving Shane and me a series of nasty, evil looks.

(Stupid children and their inability to respect travelers who are simply attempting to enjoy some romantic moments in the ocean! Grr! I fully believe children are the reason everything in life goes wrong. I have permanently given up on Freedom and Carpet and have vowed never to have children at all unless they understand that it is a major sin to publicly embarrass travelers who are simply attempting to enjoy some romantic moments in the ocean.)

We crawled out of the water – Shane quickly, and I much more grudgingly. I spent all of my remaining energy sending waves of hatred and dagger eye death stares in the direction of the small brown child the entire time.

I shielded Shane with my dress while he climbed back into his shorts. I may have (definitely) stolen another glance at his penis, which was as glorious and fantastic as I remembered. I wished I could somehow sneak a cell phone picture of his lower ab and surrounding penile area, just so I could have something to keep me warm during all the nights of total Elkton spinsterhood I had to look forward to.

Dressed again, romantic moment lost, Shane and I walked along the shoreline as the demon child and his grown up splashed about in the ocean, laughing loudly and generally being super loud and obnoxious.

"Are you with someone?" Shane asked, eyes squinty in the sunlight.

"Huh?"

"Are you with someone?" he repeated. "Do you have a boyfriend?"

"Yes," I joked. "But I enjoying traveling to romantic tropical islands by myself and making out with hot guys I meet at airport bars. You know. Keeps things fresh and all."

Shane didn't laugh. Crap. That was supposed to be funny.

"No, I'm not with anyone," I said lamely.

"Were you? I mean, before you got here?"

I wished I had another half-Xanax. Or a whole one. The situation had gone from sexy and romantic to dire and intense in the span of about fifteen seconds. I didn't know what to think, except that I really did not like situations that turned on me like that.

"Technically," I started slowly, taking a deep breath. "Technically, this is what was supposed to be, for all intents and purposes, I mean, if you were to look at the core of the situation and bypass the details, which are the most important things, you know, to be aware of, in the situation, I guess the truth is that, well, I'm technically here on my honeymoon."

I said the last part really, really fast and all in one breath, hoping he wouldn't catch the part about me being on my honeymoon.

"Your honeymoon?"

Crap.

Shane's gorgeous blue eyes went hard. I immediately felt like the sluttiest, most horrible human being who had ever lived.

"Your honeymoon," he repeated. "Wait – you were actually going to marry that guy?"

"Hey, wait a second!" My voice was shrill and came out way louder than I wanted it to.

Shane looked surprised, but I suddenly didn't care if he thought I was a bitch or a two-timer or a slut. I was tired of feeling stupid and talked down to all the time. Shane was likely the one with a non-island girlfriend anyway and was also the one who continued to act emotionally complex and difficult to figure out while providing no details about himself or his life while expecting me to share 100 percent of all my secrets with him.

"You're the one who's been acting all strange and weird!" I hissed. "Just popping out of nowhere and disappearing and popping back in again like three to five times in the last day, at least."

I was making no sense but was far too upset to notice. Until now.

"You tell me nothing about yourself," I continued. "You act emotionally confused, you probably have a non-island girlfriend somewhere back in Philadelphia, and you know an awful lot about this place for it being your first time here. So there! And, yes, this is technically my honeymoon, God*dang*it, and I'm only here by myself because my *ex*-fiancé dumped me on our wedding day. *You* found me in the airport bar, *you* liked me even though I had chicken strips on my face, *you* found my travel bag and acted all nice and cute, and you never asked what I was

ing the attacker at all. It was all so dark and everything happened so fast. He could be anyone, anywhere, waiting for me to show up, watching and waiting for another chance to spit on me and blow out my head.

A few minutes later, the old man's wife, Lupida, came to pick him up in her sky blue Jeep Wrangler. She offered to drop me back at my villa, and I graciously accepted. She was a large, robust brown woman who sang along to reggae music the whole way up Jacob's Ladder while somehow finding time to pepper me with questions about who I was and how I ended up conversing with her elderly fisherman husband, whose name, I learned, was Nico. Lupida's English was flawless, her grammar way better than mine ("I was a teacher," she boasted).

When she asked about my head, I stuck to my stupid story about night running. She *tsked tsked* and generally made me feel very loved and doted on. I wanted her to be my grandmother so bad I could cry. My own grandmother was a thin, bird-like creature who only spoke to me when she had something negative to say about the state of my hair or face, which was pretty much every day, multiple times per day. Lupida was like a warm kitchen on a cool winter morning. The first sip of coffee. The first lilac bloom you see in spring. I wanted to adopt her and wrap myself up in her arms for infinity. That would probably be a little weird, though. After awhile.

The couple let me out of their Jeep after I promised I'd go to the doctor, get some rest, drink some chicken broth, and a few other things I've already forgotten. Lupida made sure I knew where they lived just in case I needed any future help or some chicken broth ("or a hug"). I assured her I would do my very best to try and remember.

My Wrangler was still parked outside the villa, but René's had mysteriously vanished. When I poked my head in the driver's window of the Jeep (after checking the back seat, of course), I saw that the keys had been taken from the ignition. My cell phone and villa keys were gone, too. Crap.

I hobbled to the villa door, head throbbing. I had to call the cops and tell them about René the crappy caretaker so they could remove her dead hanged body from the balcony, and I could get on with my get-off-this-crazy-island-immediately plan. But all the villa doors were locked and my cell phone was MIA.

I sighed. After being almost attacked and then nearly concussed by a stupid bathroom door, I was going to have to break in to my own damn villa.

I was pretty sure my life literally could not get any worse.

I stood in the dark, trying to think up a decent break-in plan that didn't include a repeat run-in with René's bloated body. I hobbled around the entire outside perimeter (minus the dead-body-infused balcony) to better identify the potential best break-in spot, eventually discovering a largish wooden staircase off the side of the villa. With a light switch at the top. I flipped the switch, squinting in the sudden glare of the light. Then I tiptoed down the stairs and around the corner, finding a little gate leading to what I thought might be some version of an under-villa basement type thing. I didn't know if tropical islands even had basements. This one seemed to be nothing more than a dirt floor and some empty takeout bags and...what looked like a crumpled up sleeping bag? What the...was there a freaking homeless person living underneath my villa?

I was about to go investigate the weird homeless person sleeping bag situation when someone called my name.

"Sam? Is that you?"

I poked my head out from the weird under-villa area and looked up the hill. Leah was standing at the edge of the parking lot, wielding a flashlight and looking scared and relieved and very glad to see me.

"Oh thank God," she dropped her purse and rushed down the hill, nearly knocking me over with a bone-crushing bear hug. When she pulled away, her eyes were red and swimmy. "I thought..." she held me at arm's length. "Oh Sam. I'm so glad you're okay." She gave me another hug.

As you can imagine, all the hugs made me feel very loved and worthy of concern. Leah was becoming more and more like a bona fide friend and less and less like the gorgeous evil bitch of before.

She explained during our second hug how she came by to check up on me around eight o'clock after I didn't show up for dinner. She found my unlocked Jeep with the keys and my phone left inside. She'd been waiting for me ever since.

I sighed with relief, grabbing my cell phone out of her hand. "Thank you," I said. "Again. But I have to call the police. There's a dead body on my balcony."

Leah startled. "What?" she said. "You're joking, right?"

"No," I grumbled, flipping on my cell phone. (Battery: 1%; Missed Calls: 3; Callers: Kelly; Plan: ignore.) "Dammit, I have to go plug this in. My battery's empty."

"Um...Sam," Leah said as I started limping up the hill. "Are you okay?"

As I walked toward the front door, I thought about my almost concussed head, my emotional damage, and the dead hanged body I'd seen. I could never un-see René's green swollen face. It would be there for the rest of my life, waiting for me in my nightmares.

"Never better," I mumbled in response to Leah's question. Tears pricked my eyes.

"So...you were joking about the body, right?"

"Go look for yourself," I told her. "Someone killed my crappy caretaker."

"René?" Leah startled again. "Oh my God!"

She ran around to the balcony, then stomped back over to me.

"You're sick," she spat. "That is *not* funny."

"What?" I stopped fumbling with my keys and peered around the corner.

René was gone.

"But..." I looked at Leah. "But I saw her."

"When?"

"Earlier tonight," I said. "I swear. Before I was..."

I rushed back to the parking lot. There was no trace of René's Wrangler, no proof that she'd been there at all.

"But..."

I could tell Leah didn't believe me. "I was here the whole time, Sam," she said. "I came here around eight, after you didn't show for dinner. There was no one here."

"Didn't you see her Jeep though? It was parked right here..."

Leah shook her head slowly.

"But..." My knees went wobbly and everything went all spinny. I stumbled.

Leah grabbed my elbow and steered me to the front door. She helped me unlock the door and hobble into the villa, knees knocking. I collapsed onto the futon. My body trembled.

"You've been through a lot," Leah said gently. "Bumped your head...maybe you should go see a doctor?"

"I don't want to go to a doctor," I mumbled. "I know what I saw."

Leah looked at me warily.

"I'm fine," I said. Outside, the winds picked up and the skies opened. Rain beat heavy on the roof.

Leah grabbed me a fluffy towel. I wrapped it around myself and burst into a fresh set of tears.

"This place sucks!" I wailed. "I'm going home!"

Leah tucked me into her shoulder and let me cry on what was probably multi-billion dollar designer fabric of some sort.

"Shh," she said, patting me on the back. "It's alright. Tell me what happened."

I told her about finding René, about the attacker in my backseat, the death rag, the stinky breath, the gun, and the bathroom door.

"Oh Sam," she said. Her face was pale. She gave me another hug. "I'm so sorry I –" she faltered. "I'm just so sorry."

I informed Leah of my plans to return home immediately and had to endure her subsequent beggings to stay and enjoy the rest of my un-honeymoon. I argued that my very frightening blood-hungry almost-attacker was still on the island somewhere, knew where I was staying, and would likely return to the villa and kill me at his first opportunity. My only real hope was to get really far away, immediately. As far away as I could. Immediately.

Leah argued, convincingly, that the ferry was probably closed due to the storm and we were all stranded anyway, so why not use the opportunity to head to a non-sweaty, attacker-free place with hot water and cable television and free spa treatments?

Long story short, we compromised and agreed that I would pack my stuff, stay with Leah temporarily and, after a long hot shower and power nap, I would enjoy a day of rest and relaxation that would include a whole body massage with exfoliation and hot rocks, a facial, and the mysterious eyebrow threads, among other free-makeover type things.

After the ferry re-opened and my emotional status had re-balanced, I would reconsider my options and speak with an island therapist if needed. (Leah happened to have an on-call island therapist on speed dial but, unfortunately, did not know any island sorceresses who specialized in breaking curses.)

Leah asked if I wanted to go to the police station and tell them about René and my attacker. I thought of Officer Gregory. Of my last visit. Of feeling like a joke. I imagined going back with stories about a dead body that wasn't there and an attacker I never actually saw and could never identify in a line up because all I knew about him was that he had the same accent as pretty much everyone else who lives on the island. Right.

Instead, I suggested a post-makeover pig-out on pizza and cheesy garlic bread.

Done.

So I'm signing off to pack up my stuff and move my life from my sweaty un-safe villa while taking rejuvenating steps toward emotional and physical post-almost-attacked health.

Until next time. (No comments, please.)

Date: Tuesday
Time: 6:20 p.m.
Location: Blissful Days Day Spa.
Day Rating (So Far): Four stars. Successful post-almost-attack rebound in full effect.

I am a glorious, gorgeous, attractive-looking beach goddess! Compared to before, anyway. I cannot stop looking at myself in the mirror. I cannot stop shaking my bangs and "micro-layers" and smiling at everything and everyone. My life is once again wonderful and filled with miraculous makeovers and new, very good bangs! I truly believe my earlier curse has expired, as the last 24 hours have included such wondrous things as: escape from a possible dead body, post-almost-attack survival, *and* a successful free makeover. That sort of thing doesn't happen to just anyone, especially people who have curses on them.

Time: 7:15 p.m.
Location: Blissful Days Day Spa.

Note to past self: I should have gotten a free makeover eons ago. Like when I was born. My entire life leading up to this point would have been so much better, and I would have felt way better overall about the state of myself, my hair, and my face. Therefore, I would have had more self-confidence, gotten a better education, moved out of Elkton, and never gotten dumped by Colin. Therefore, I never would have been almost-attacked or hit by a bathroom door. I highly recommend this course of action to anyone trying to decide between getting a free makeover and not getting a free makeover. Hurrah!

My day at Leah's spa has been the best overall day of my whole entire life thus far. I'm obviously still pretty damaged by the almost-attacking and subsequent near-death situation via bathroom door, but my reluctant two-hour discussion with Leah's on-call therapist has resulted in a willingness to accept, let go, and move forward with both my life and my attitude. And a commitment to think about maybe thinking about someday accepting the possibility that I might have a slightly unhealthy Xanax addiction. Maybe.

I have learned that the recipe for successful post-almost-attack recovery includes the following:

- Multiple variations of prescription pharmaceutical and wine combinations (treatment of possible unhealthy Xanax addiction to begin at a later date).
- Four hour nap.

- Super hot shower complete with very hot water and spendy, good-smelling shower products.
- Lunch of cheese and baguette and wine like a true foreign goddess.
- Emphasis on the wine/prescription pharmaceuticals.

In case you hadn't heard, the free makeover Leah and her spa team gave me was a 100 percent complete and total success. I have actually succeeded in going from a pale freckled Midwesterner with a very poor state of hair and face to a glowy spray-tanned islander with flowy highlighted layers, sexy bangs, and artificially darkened eyelashes. I generally feel much more positive about the state of my hair and face overall and no longer look like a woman version of Clay Aiken. Hurrah!

During my free makeover, Leah's super helpful spa team ensured that my skin became soft and exfoliated and spray tanned to glowy perfection. My nails were groomed and painted a shimmery island pink with my cuticles pushed back appropriately. My teeth were bleached and blasted until they became ultra-white and completely stain-free and dazzling. My eyebrow threading became whole-face threading and the entire area has gone from a hairy overgrown forest to general smooth silkiness. My eyelashes and eyebrows were tinted to give the appearance of having more and better eyelashes and eyebrows than I actually have. My hair was highlighted and trimmed into millions of micro-layers that cascade from head to shoulders and look generally flirty and highly awesome. My bangs were cut all long and sexy and are very shakeable. They also do a very successful job of disguising my tall, wide forehead and my temple gouge. My makeup was applied by someone who knows lots about makeup and the whole resulting look is one of general, effortless sexiness. (I did decide to politely decline the hair extensions due to having very strong feelings about wearing phony hair and hesitations around false advertising of my true attractiveness level. Plus, my regular hair looks amazing enough for now.)

I never, ever want to look any different than this. I mean, I would probably eventually like to be taller but, otherwise, I have current total satisfaction re: my new hair and face, especially my dark lashes and forehead disguising bangs.

I've figured that, even if the attacker reunion becomes imminent, the attacker is not likely to recognize now-me as past-me and is likely to walk right by and try to attack someone else instead. I also feel very proficient at my post-second chance life re-do since I have already successfully completed two items on my Universe/Jesus promise list!

The only things left to do are:

- New personality and attitude (am working on this per therapy call).
- More initiative around being a positive contributor to society and human race in general.
- New job that is not located in, on, or anywhere near Elkton.
- New boss that has normal name for gender and isn't a huge dick asshole who calls and annoys me on my un-honeymoon.
- More cruciferous vegetables and less Xanax.

I will start the rest of my list as soon as I get back home. For now, my plan is to consume my entire weight in pepperoni pizza and cheesy garlic bread, drink enough wine to lapse into nightmare-free unconsciousness, and probably eventually dig up a box of Oreos and my *Love Actually* DVD because, really, it just feels so good.

Date: Wednesday
Time: 7:15 a.m.
Location: Leah's Villa/Joe's Diner.
Day Rating (So Far): Awesome new look = amazing; recent mysterious discoveries in Leah's villa = highly unsettling.

I woke up way too early and watched the most beautiful sunrise from my king-sized bed (which is, by far, *the* most comfortable bed I've ever slept on in my life) through Leah's floor-to-ceiling mansion windows. Somehow, Leah is not only gorgeous and an amazing spa-owner/makeover artist, but she is also very incredibly and awesomely wealthy. I'm pretty sure her weekend-only spa doesn't generate nearly enough revenue to support the purchase of a mansion villa on a tropical island, despite the very desirable lack of island income tax. She must be a trust fund baby or the lucky recipient of a massive inheritance from a wealthy relative or something. Dammit! I wish I was a trust fund baby or the lucky recipient of a massive inheritance from a wealthy relative or something. The only things I'll inherit from my relatives are shitty Elkton mortgage payments and some old bedazzled sweatshirts. Stupid.

Anyway, after enjoying a very proper lie-in, I realized I was ravenous despite my recent massive carb consumption. So I got up to poke around for something to eat.

Leah's island mansion was so enormous, I felt the need to do some proper snooping and give myself a proper tour, seeing as we were both so drunk on wine and Oreos and full on pizza and *Love Actually* by the time we got to the mansion last night that we basically just said goodnight and crashed. Good thing Leah's spa is only a five minute walk from her mansion and it only took us about twenty drunken minutes to get from there to here.

The guest room I was crashing in was at the end of a long, wide hallway with doors on either side. As I snooped around, I poked my nose into each of the open rooms, finding a bathroom (which I patronized), a study, and a smaller second guest room. (Because everyone needs more than one guest room.) There was also a ginormous kitchen filled with granite countertops and stainless steel appliances and a whole other wing that held a library, a laundry room, and a set of double doors at the end of a long hallway that surely led to Leah's master suite.

After toasting a bagel in the stainless steel toaster oven and smearing some honey nut cream cheese all over it, I poked around in the library a bit, checking out the dusty collection of ancient names and titles intermixed with modern thrillers, legal mysteries, and chick lit.

I soon discovered that Leah was in possession of an 1866 first edition copy of *Alice's Adventures in Wonderland* by Lewis Carroll in near-perfect condition. In case you didn't know, an 1866 first edition copy of *Alice's Adventures in Wonderland* by Lewis Carroll in near-perfect condition is worth like ten thousand dollars! At least! I know this because Elkton librarian Martha Shaker has a super weirdo obsession with crusty old books and is practically in love with her stupid copy of *Alice's Adventures in Wonderland* which has a big grease stain on the cover and is missing some pages. I had to hear at least a hundred times how much that dumb book would be worth if it didn't have the grease stain on the cover and all the missing pages. I'd bet Martha Shaker would build a shrine to her book if it were in better condition. She would probably worship it on a multi-daily basis. And here Leah had her practically perfect copy casually tucked into her bookcase next to the latest John Grisham best-seller like it was no big thing. I may or may not have gotten nervous and dropped the book and then got some honey nut cream cheese on the cover when I picked it back up. But it only left a little smudge. No biggie.

Anyway, the spendy rare book wasn't what unsettled me and caused me to sneak out of the mansion immediately. What unsettled me and caused me to sneak out of the mansion immediately was what I found lying on top of Leah's coffee table after I accidentally smeared cream cheese all over her spendy rare book and was looking for a place to safely stow my bagel while I wiped my sticky fingers.

On top of Leah's coffee table, right under the latest copy of *Italian Vogue* magazine, sat a stack of photos. Of me.

Let me say that again.

Leah had a stack of freaking pictures. Of me. Randomly taken during my last few days on the island. There were a few from my first night at the Beached Bar, talking with Jimmy and drinking with Shane. There were a couple from when I was walking around the island the next day by myself – just before or after I left the police station. There were even a few of my oceanic escapade with Shane! At the bottom of the stack, I found at least half a dozen close-up shots of my formerly un-special un-engagement ring.

What. The. Hell.

And that's not all I found, either. As I was subsequently digging around in a closet for a travel bag to use to pack up some of my stuff and quickly escape Leah and her scary voyeuristic photo habits, I came across my missing underpants lying right on top of a pile of dirty laundry! Aaagh!

That's right. My missing underpants – the ones I lost during my first fateful drunken night on the island – were lying in Leah's dirty laundry basket.

I threw some clothes and my nasty purse into a random travel bag, scribbled a note to Leah, and left the villa. By this point, I was sweating profusely and feeling very vomitous in both my stomach and my head. My headache was also back with a serious vengeance. I wished I'd had the forethought to bring more pharmaceutical drugs and wine.

What sort of person takes sneaky pictures of another person and has another person's underpants in her dirty laundry basket? I can't even begin to understand how Leah came across my underpants in the first place and/or why, if she did come across them, she felt the need to pick them up, bring them home, and put them in her dirty laundry for everyone to see.

Being newly awesome looks-wise and very quick minded and confident, I have already thought through and discarded a dozen possible underpants-stealing explanations while writing them down in my official 007 clue remembering notebook:

1. I gave Leah my underpants to hold while we were in the bathroom during my first drunken night on the island. (This is very unlikely as I generally don't like to pass dirty underpants to complete strangers to hold, even when in a state of massive drunkenness.)
2. Leah stole my underpants from me so she could bring them home and throw them into her dirty laundry. (This is also unlikely as I generally don't allow strangers to take off my underpants…unless the stranger's name is Shane and he has a penis the size of New Hampshire.)
3. Leah randomly found my underpants lying on the ground and picked them up to bring them home and throw them into her

dirty laundry. (Unless Leah possesses a strange dirty-underpants fetish, this is probably also very unlikely.)

4. And the most likely but still very unlikely explanation: I took off the underpants and stuffed them into my purse. Leah found my purse and took out the underpants to bring home and throw in her dirty laundry. Perhaps she did this as a favor so she could return the clean underpants to me at a later time? Still, this is a very weak argument and generally very unsettling to think about, as what sort of person washes the underpants of a drunken tourist stranger just to be nice?

None of these explanations did an adequate enough job of also explaining why Leah had a stack of a dozen sneaky pictures of me in various poses and various stages of drunkenness sitting there on her coffee table under her *Italian Vogue* for all the world to see. With close ups of the ring that magically disappeared during my first night on the island.

All I know is that I felt way too weird about the whole thing to just sit there in the villa and wait for her to wake up so I could ask her about it. I mean, how does one go about asking a brand new friend (who has just given one a successful free makeover) if perhaps the friend may have taken a bunch of sneaky photos of one and also stolen one's underpants?

In addition, how does one explain that one found these items because one was snooping around the house while the friend was sleeping? And also that one may have smudged the friend's million dollar antique book?

Right. Definitely not awkward at all. So I decided to do what I do with all issues involving confrontation: avoid it.

Now I'm at Joe's Diner, eating breakfast by myself. (Yes, I was still hungry after my bagel cream cheese; I am on vacation where diets do not exist.) I'm currently sitting at a corner stool overlooking Cruz Bay, wondering about the general strangeness of life on this very weird and beautiful romantic tropical island.

Since I have nothing better to do and am deathly afraid of going back to my attacker-infested sweaty villa, I have courageously decided that today is the day I will head across the sea via island ferry to visit Sapphire Junction, the St. Thomas jewelry shop from the magazine ad I ripped out on the plane. There, I will have a proper conversation with the shop manager in hopes the discussion will lead to another clue about the missing ring situation. Afterwards, I will use all the clues to solve the ring mission, recover my ring, and go home before Leah wakes up and/or the attacker can find me.

Good plan.

Because my almost-attacking, René's disappearing dead body, and the free makeover were very, very distracting (as was the recovery of my missing underpants and the discovery of the illicit photos taken of me behind my back), I've been feeling very distracted and off-track with my ring detection mission. I have to remember that I have only four days left on my un-honeymoon, and I have to pick up my pace like now if I have any chance of solving the case in the nick of time. Like a true 007. A very poor 007 with no real skills in any area whatsoever. Except a winning mental attitude. Some of the time, anyway. Or none of the time.

I also need to figure out my wallet-return game plan with my sexy suspicious character, Shane, so I can at least get one sexual episode out of him before having to head home. I mean, the whole point of our massive flirtation and ocean make out session was to enjoy round-the-clock romantic island sex, right? I refuse to give up without a valiant last-ditch final attempt at seeing and fully experiencing both his abs and his lower ab area. I plan to either act aloof and hard to get during the wallet exchange or rip his clothes off and jump all over him. (Will let situation unfold naturally.) I also have to break the news that my sausage-armed attacker stole all his wallet dollars. I'm not quite sure how that whole conversation is going to go.

In reviewing my ring evidence and updating my sleuthing notebook, I've added sausage-arms to my list of suspects, removed the likely-dead but maybe not René, and added the following clues to my mission evidence/facts:

- Both Leah and the attacker referred to my ring as a *diamond* ring. I am quite sure Colin would not have felt the need to explain why he "designed" a garnet ring instead of a diamond ring if, in fact, it was a diamond ring all along. I would definitely ask the jewelry shop to clarify, as this is quite an important distinction.

- Also, since the attacker asked me where the ring was, this likely means he did not know, himself, where the ring was. Or else he would not have asked me about it. So either he is not the ring thief or he is the ring thief and had someone steal the ring from me except that person disappeared with the ring instead of giving the ring to the attacker.

- Since Leah had numerous close-up photos of my ring, she obviously has a high level of interest in the ring; perhaps she has been the ring stealer this whole time. But then why offer to help me look for it and then get all weirded out by the magazine ad? It just doesn't make any sense.

I am getting so good at clue collecting, my head is spinning. There are too many clues and not enough clue-solving. Must remember to get better at clue-solving. (Note to future self: get better at clue-solving.)

Hopefully my trip to Sapphire Junction will result in even more clues and all the evidence and clue-solving answers I need to support the quick and successful completion of my ring-detecting mission.

(As you can see, I am attempting to change my attitude and live on the sunny side of life per my second-chance-at-life Universe/Jesus promise list. It's a wonder what a free makeover and a two-hour therapy session can do for one's emotional state. My new look, so far, has proved to be the most glorious, triumphant life addition ever. Despite my recent near-death episode and other general awfulness, I continue to feel that life is generally very precious and not worth wasting one bit.)

My second breakfast of bacon and eggs with a mound of cheesy potatoes has arrived, so I am off to indulge my post-death un-honeymoon appetite and wink at the sexy waiter who may or may not be flirting with me heavily. Hurrah to all the flirting!

Comment from Anonymous: Interesting perspective on near-death experiences, although many people need more than short-term therapy and prescription medication to recover completely. Check out a few other ways to treat post near-death depression in my blog, The Psychologically Healthy Human's, latest article Post Near-Death Depression: The Slow, Quiet Killer. You are not alone.

P.S. Must remember to figure out how to disable comments.

Date: Wednesday
Time: Noonish
Location: Very mysterious island of St. Thomas, sitting in non-air conditioned bistro stuffing my face with chocolate croissants and feeling generally confused and very upset about everything.
Day Rating (So Far): Three mediocre stars.

Pros: My new makeover look has tremendously increased my overall life success. The whole bangs/cascading hair situation makes walking a very fun and bouncy affair. I've also uncovered the most amazing ring clues to boot!
Cons: I've made a secondary unsettling discovery regarding my ex-fiancé and my suspicious island friend and want to throw both of them into the middle of the ocean ASAP. It seems that unsettling discoveries lie around every corner. I'm now generally disinterested in looking around any other corners.

After leaving the villa mansion and its underpants-stealing sneaky-picture-taking owner behind, I successfully ferried myself and my new flirty bangs to the steamy island of St. Thomas. My main goal for the venture across the sea was to visit Sapphire Junction, the crappy touristy jewelry shop located near Sapphire Bay, just a few cab ride minutes away from the Red Hook ferry dock.

There was nothing of note to report on the St. Thomas-bound ferry besides a general lack of attacker-looking individuals and a noticeable increase in the number of smiles and stares from strange men and only stares from strange women.

I'm pretty sure my new sexy long bangs that frame my eyes and brush my cheekbones at the sides have magically turned my face from a five to a forehead-concealed seven and, paired with my sexy glowing skin and very white teeth and cascading highlights and long dark lashes, I could maybe even pass for an eight in the right (very dim) light. Hurrah! This was all very nice and life-changing, and I discovered that I truly enjoyed bouncing around with my highlights and peeking up at people with my dark lashes from under my longish bangs. I've become a true believer in the powers of expensively revolutionary spa treatments and vow to find a way to continue with the eyebrow threading and bang-cutting for the rest of my life, even if it means traveling to St. John once per month to have Leah do it for free. If I ever talk to her again. Which I won't. Unless she has a socially acceptable explanation for her behavior as of late. Which I doubt.

Anyway, although the ferry ride was less than interesting, things took a turn for the very interesting indeed as soon as I caught a cab at Red Hook.

"Where are you headed?" the cab driver asked after I climbed into the backseat. He was a dark man with a gray beard and thick blackish-gray dreadlocks, wearing a pit stained white button down shirt. His cab smelled like sweat and warm ear wax.

"It's called Sapphire Junction," I replied. "It's a jewelry store near Sapphire Bay."

"Sure, sure," said the driver. "I know Sapphire Junction."

"Great," I replied, glad I wouldn't have to attempt to navigate us there, as that would likely turn into a horribly embarrassing scenario where I revealed my inability to follow GPS and read street signs.

"But it's no jewelry store, love," the driver continued, pulling onto Route 32 and hammering on the gas.

(See? Case in point. No one has ever called me 'love' before in casual conversation. I mean, I've heard of it happening before and have also seen it in movies, of course. But it had never happened to pre-bang me.)

"Wait. What did you say?" I finally registered what the driver said after moving past the 'love' comment.

"It's no jewelry store, I said," said the driver.

"Sapphire Junction?" I pulled out the now-worn half magazine ad and checked again. "Yeah, Sapphire Junction. The jewelry store." I shoved the ad in his face and shook my bangs at him. "See?"

"Yes, I see it there, love." (Swoon.) "But, that's Sapphire

Junction, the museum, you're thinking of."

My cell phone buzzed while I was unsuccessfully attempting to register both the new non-jewelry shop information and the two love comments put together. It was all slightly too much to handle. The caller was Kelly, of course, for the eightieth time, and I declined his call immediately.

Sigh.

Then my phone buzzed with a text message. It read:

Sam, Kelly here. Understand your wedding did not go as planned. Need to speak ASAP. Expect call back within hour. Kelly.

He must have hit the send button twice, because the same exact message came through not five seconds later.

Sigh. Again. I deleted both texts immediately and pretended they never existed at all. Why does Kelly have to be such a huge dick all the time?

Just so everyone knows, my boss Kelly is a giant behemoth of a man-child who used to be a lowly postal worker but somehow got a job in middle management at Peterson's Meat Packing. Then, somehow, he got promoted. Probably because he glad-handled the owner's balls and kissed his ass all day long. Then he somehow got promoted again. Then he became my boss. Then my life was basically ruined over and over again Monday through Friday.

Kelly has very long dark hair that he wears tied back in a ponytail and, every day, he wears jeans, a blazer, and suede cowboy boots with spurs on them. He pulls his jeans up so high that you can literally see the outline of his...well, you know. He spends all day sitting in meetings and swaggering around the plant talking about how great he is and ignoring how much everyone hates him. Plus, he makes me come in every Monday at 7am for a stupid HR meeting that he's always late for. But if I'm late, he gives me a write up and puts it in my employment file. Plus, he calls me all the time. Like five times a day. Even on nights and weekends. And on my un-honeymoon, the only vacation I've ever taken since I started working at Peterson's

Meat Packing. Kelly also talks about everyone behind their backs and just fired poor Trudy, our receptionist, for disagreeing with him in a meeting. Even though Trudy had been with Peterson's for 14 years and knew everything about everything. Now I get to do Trudy's job in addition to my own with no extra pay or a change in job title or cubicle size.

In short, working for Kelly is the pits. The absolute worst. I HATE HIM!!

In any case, back to the cab situation. And sorry for the emotional side note. Sort of.

My attempts to handle all the information regarding the museum vs. jewelry shop, the cab driver's love comments, the call from Kelly, his subsequent text messages demanding a call back within the hour, and my recovering from the almost attack all failed miserably. It was all just way too much to bear, so I popped a half Xanax (a whole one) and tried to figure out what to do next.

Obviously I would not be calling Kelly back. First off, I hated him with all my might and, secondly, I did not appreciate getting calls and texts on my un-honeymoon for something that would certainly end up being a stupid non-emergency.

He was probably calling to get an update on the upcoming launch of the company's annual performance review process, and I refused to be forced into speaking with him and hearing his horrible voice while on vacation. Plus everyone hates performance reviews and thinks they are stupid and a monster waste of time. No one ever gets any raises because Kelly takes all the extra merit pool money for his own bonus. And he just bought a fancy yacht that he stores on Lake Wabagosha for everyone to see. Meanwhile, everyone else makes do with their meager slave wages that don't even keep up with inflation.

Plus, in case you didn't know, I am a attack survivor now, practically, and therefore don't care if Kelly fires me. In fact, I hope he does. I hope he fires me so I can go on unemployment and not have to look at his stupid camel tail and listen to his stupid voice all day every day.

Hey Kelly, if you're reading this, I've got a response to your text message. It's even within the hour, as requested. FUCK. YOU. Fuck You. Fuuuuuck Yooouuuuu. I hate you.

Okay, I'm really done now, I promise.

Moving on.

"A museum?" I said finally, after I realized the cab driver was staring at me in the rearview mirror like I was a crazy tourist who yelled obscenities at her cell phone. I decided at that moment to officially forget about Kelly and his demanding text messages and move on to more exciting things, like ring-detecting and conversing with the owner of a non-jewelry store museum.

"What kind of museum?" I wondered out loud. Natural history? Geological? Wax? I wondered if that critical piece of information was lost in the half of the ad I hadn't ripped out of the magazine. It probably was.

The driver pulled up to a squat building with pearl-colored walls and a flat, warm brown slate roof. Five oblong half-circle windows spanned the entire front of the building like arches. The middle window was actually a door, and the whole thing looked like it belonged in some sort of Japanese Zen garden.

"It's an art museum," the driver replied. "The biggest art museum on the island. See for yourself, love."

I hopped out, grinning at the multiple love comments and his confusion over art museum vs. art gallery terminology.

The cab ride had taken like three minutes and was only a few bucks, but I gave the driver a tenner from my rapidly dwindling supply of dollars, mainly because of the love comments and subsequent boost to my self-esteem. I wished I'd had the opportunity to steal all of Shane's suspicious wallet-dollars before the stupid attacker took them. That would have made my life tons easier.

The cab left me staring at the museum/gallery door which, when I tried it, was locked. It was still very early, and I figured the place wasn't open yet, so I sat on a bench and doodled in my sleuthing notebook, reviewing my clues and thinking about the disappearing ring mystery.

What really bothered me was how the attacker knew my name. I mean, I know the island is small and everything, but I thought only a few people knew me – René, Shane, Leah, Jimmy, and the policeman Office Gregory. Did one of them see me with the ring and tip off sausage arms? Was there some cahooting going on and, if so, who was part of the cahooting and who was trustworthy? I really hoped Shane was trustworthy. Despite the contents of his wallet and all his suspicious phone calls and weird emotional issues. I just really wanted to sleep with him over and over until I had go back home and sleep with no one ever again. I couldn't really do that if he was the ring stealer, could I?

Each of the suspects was odd in his or her own personal way – René with her fast talking and possible drug habit and disappearing dead body trick, Shane with his emotional bipolarism and mysterious phone conversations and lack of wallet contents, Leah with her underpants fetish and sneaky photo taking, Jimmy for dating a chick with an underpants fetish and for looking at me weird and for his unnaturally green eyes, and the policeman for his odd reaction to the ad and his generally unhelpful and shoddy actions.

In any case, someone must have told someone who must have told someone who told the attacker, or something like that. It was all too much for my post-almost-concussed, slightly hung over brain.

I eventually got tired of thinking and waiting for the museum gallery to open, so I walked up to the middle window that was actually a door and tried the handle. It was still locked, as closed buildings usually are, so I peered through the glass, cupping my hands around my eyes to see inside.

The museum was deserted except for a young girl who stood behind a desk, counting a stack of bills. She mouthed numbers to herself as she counted, making neat piles of money on the counter. A strand of brown hair fell over her eyes and she shook it away, losing count and starting all over again.

I tapped my knuckles softly on the glass to try and get her attention.

"Hello?" I called, tapping louder. She didn't look up.

"Hello?" I said again, even louder.

"Can I help you?" said a voice behind me.

I jumped and spun around, shaking my bangs and feeling highly embarrassed and voyeuristic. A short, thin man in a taupe suit that almost matched the museum gallery walls stood in front of me. He held a key in one freckly wrinkled hand and a dark brown briefcase in the other. His head was nearly bald except for a furry patch of white hair above each ear, and he wore wire spectacles that made perfect circles around his swimmy brown eyes.

"Do you work here?" I asked.

The man nodded. "We don't open for an hour," he explained. "But there's a little bistro about a block from here where you can grab some coffee and wait, if you like."

I didn't want any coffee, and I certainly didn't want to wait, so I ignored him and decided to shake my bangs and follow him inside.

(Note to future self: new bangs are a magical source of infinite confidence and power; must remember to always keep bangs exactly like they are now. Always.)

The man unlocked the door, swung it open, and walked inside. I followed behind him, thinking about my highlights and feeling very confident, despite the wary looks the man kept tossing my way.

We walked into a large, rectangle room cluttered with pedestals and display cases. Paintings filled the bright white walls as far as the eye could see.

The girl from the front desk stopped counting and looked up. "You made me lose my place," she complained. Then, "Who is that?"

Her voice was like sandpaper against my newly threaded chin. I hated her right away.

"Miss," the old man said patiently as he turned to face me. "We're closed. I'm sorry, but you'll just have to come back later."

I pulled the half-ad out from my purse and showed it to him. "I just have a few questions," I said. "About the ring."

The man's face turned ashen when he glanced at the ad. He tightened his grip on his briefcase, pursed his lips, and leaned in toward me. "I already answered all your questions," he whispered harshly, nearly spitting directly into my face. I sighed. I was starting to get very sick of people spitting on me all the time.

"What questions?" I asked him. "What are you talking about?"

"You're a reporter, right? Miss…"

"Stone," I replied, extending my hand for him to shake. His grip was weak, his hand super soft and gross and clammy. "Samantha Stone," I added with a smile. (A small one.) I never called myself Samantha, but it felt right and sounded very confident and balanced. "And I'm no reporter." I flashed a bigger smile and a bang-shake.

The man softened and gave me a wan, tight-lipped smile. "The police, then?"

I shook my head. "No, not the police."

His face opened. "Ah," he said. "E.J. must have sent you."

"E.J." I said. "Sure. E.J. Whatever. Look, sir. I'm just trying to find some answers. If you don't mind. I mean, I could come back when the gallery opens, but I would hate to disrupt you during business hours."

The man sighed, gesturing for me to follow him. "Very well," he said softly.

I felt a little bad for him, being so old and still having to work. They must not have retirement programs on St. Thomas like we have in America. Lame.

The man walked diagonally across the rectangle room toward a small office tucked near the back corner. Our footsteps echoed loudly in the empty hall. When we entered the office, the man set his briefcase on the desk and pulled out a chair for me. He sat behind the desk and flipped on the computer monitor.

"I am Mr. Hanson," the man said. "Harold Hanson." He opened a window on his computer screen. "I manage Sapphire Junction."

"Nice to meet you, Mr. Hanson," I replied. "Thank you for seeing me."

He chuckled. "As if you gave me a choice, Miss Stone," he said wryly.

I smiled and shook my bangs. Damn right, I thought. I'm an

attack survivor. I also dodged a concussion. And I just got a really successful free makeover. I don't take 'no' for an answer from no one.

"Why did you think I was a reporter?" I asked.

Hanson paused. "After the...incident," he paused again, his cheeks going red. "There were so many reporters. They've dwindled over the months, but I still get at least one a week."

Art galleries and incidents and reporters...things were starting to make lots more sense. I was starting to believe that I may be the unwilling party to something very awful and horrendously illegal. I started stress sweating right away.

"Tell me about the... incident," I said, flapping my elbows to try and air out my pits.

"I can't tell you anything more than what was in the news," Hanson argued wearily.

I obviously had no idea what he was talking about since I hadn't been following St. John/St. Thomas news as a general practice. So I successfully deployed my mission-confident 007 interrogation techniques, and I'm happy to report that they worked like a charm.

"Mr. Hanson," I said patiently. "I'd like to hear it from you." I sounded very firm and confident and slightly argumentative.

"Well," Hanson sighed. "Where should I begin?"

"The very beginning," I said. "Tell me everything."

I took my sleuthing notebook out of my purse and flipped it open. Hanson watched me silently. I looked up, raising a shapely eyebrow and shaking my bangs.

"Whenever you're ready, Mr. Hanson."

"This is a very long story," Hanson sighed. "I'll need a glass of water." He gestured to a small water cooler in the corner of the room. Then he sat and stared at me.

After a few moments of staring back and forth at each other, I eventually realized that the old man actually wanted *me* to get *him* a glass of water, like I was, once again, some sort of personal slave and he was some sort of very old person who was used to having personal slaves pour water for him. But, since I wanted answers to all my great questions, being a water-fetching butler for a minute seemed like a decently okay trade.

After I filled up a glass that was sitting next to the cooler, I set it on the desk in front of him and sat back down.

"I'm ready, Mr. Hanson."

Hanson sighed and leaned back in his chair. Actually, he leaned a little *too* far back and nearly lost his balance. It took all my powers not to laugh. I reminded myself that I was supposed to be sleuthing and that sleuthing was very serious business. I swallowed my laugh and started coughing.

Hanson took a small sip of water and turned to his computer, typing quickly. After I recovered from my laugh-coughing episode, I leaned forward to see what he'd pulled up on the screen. I found myself looking at the image of a triangular red stone. Beneath the stone, it read "The DeBlume Red."

"The DeBlume Red is the fourth largest red diamond in the world," Hanson explained. "3.03 carats." He pointed to the screen. "Some call it a trillion or trilliant cut," his voice dropped. "It was so beautiful. A red stone with a slightly brownish hue. It was actually mistaken for a garnet for many years."

He paused, taking another sip of water. He moved like a turtle, all slow and old. It was hard for me to keep my patience. I took a deep breath, trying to remember all the sleuthing and 007 techniques I'd learned from the movies.

"In the mid-19th century, as the story goes, a man called Louis Vitale won the stone in a game of poker." Hanson kept staring at the screen, talking very slowly and elderly-like. "The man who bet it," he continued, "Frederick von Huessen, believed it was a garnet. It wasn't until Vitale had it appraised that he learned it was a red diamond. An exceedingly rare red diamond. Vitale commissioned his cousin to design a ring setting worthy of the stone and, once the setting was complete, Vitale traveled from Italy to Spain to ask for his love's hand in marriage. She accepted, of course, and the two lived happily just outside Rome for many years. History has it that the ring passed to the first born of each generation. It now belongs to Francisco Vitale. Or did."

"Did?" I asked curiously.

"Have you not read the papers, Detective Stone?"

(Did you catch that? He called me *detective*. As in awesome and very 007! I must remember to act very important and detectively. Also, I did not correct him.)

"Of course I've read the papers," I said confidently. (I have not read the papers.) "However, I believe the story, coming directly from the source, provides much more...*depth* of information...than does a simple news bit." I said it flippantly, shaking my bangs and highlights around a bit.

"Of course, my apologies, Detective Stone."

Apologies not accepted. "Tell me about the ring. Where is it now?"

Hanson gave me a puzzled look. "Well, that is the million dollar question, is it not? Two-point-two million dollars, to be exact."

Er – right.

"Mr. Vitale graciously loaned the ring to Sapphire Junction for our grand re-opening last spring," Hanson said. "We had it on display for just a week before it was stolen." He pulled open another screen and I found myself staring at a picture of the ring from the ad. The ring that was stolen. *My* ring.

All the blood rushed to my head. I gripped the arms of my chair to keep from falling over. I couldn't believe it. I'd been wearing an ancient and rare (and stolen) red diamond ring for months. My stomach turned. I nearly barfed all over Hanson's desk. I wore that ring while showering, while sleeping, while digging in the garbage disposal, while baking and cooking. I'd gotten mashed potatoes and lotion trapped inside it. I didn't clean it one time. I never sent in the insurance paperwork. I really don't think there ever *was* insurance paperwork. Because it was stolen. Stolen by my – oh *God.*

(What was Colin thinking?! Stealing a 3.03 carat red diamond ring from a St. Thomas art gallery and then letting me travel to St. John for my honeymoon while wearing the same 3.03 carat red diamond ring. No wonder I was almost attacked! I hate Colin and all men in general for constantly making such horrible, life-altering decisions. Aagh!)

Hanson was staring at me again. The look on my face as I realized I'd been flashing a fancy stolen ring around everywhere must have included large bulbous eyes, red cheeks, a dropped jaw, and lots and lots of forehead stress sweating.

"Uh. Um. Er... Ho–How was it stolen Mr. Harold?" I asked

through my stress sweating. "I mean, Mr. Harold. Handle. *Hanson.*"

God! I scolded myself. Get it together! I flapped my elbows again and tried to breathe.

"It was stolen during the auction," Hanson explained, eyeing me suspiciously. "We have one every May, you see, to sell off our existing pieces and make way for new ones. An artist stopped by at the end of the night, right after we closed, to pick up the pieces that hadn't sold at the auction. I was in the back with him while, out front, someone broke into the display and took the ring."

"You didn't hear anything while you were in the back?"

Hanson gave me the same wary look. "Of course," he said slowly. "The alarms went off. But, as the papers stated, I was locked in the back with the artist while the robbery occurred. We weren't found until the police arrived and let us out. By that time, it was too late. The ring was gone."

"Is there any camera footage?" I asked. "Security tapes?" I congratulated myself for not only pulling my emotions together but also for asking such awesome and detectively sounding questions.

Hanson nodded slowly. "The police have them," he said, taking another sip of water. It took a year for him to get the glass from the table to his face. He was so old and slow. I felt so bad for him. Sort of.

"However," he croaked. "The camera lenses had been shattered, so I'm not certain that what footage they do have is of any help at all."

"What have the police found?"

"Up until now," Hanson's eyes went more swimmy. "They've found nothing. Nothing at all."

"Nor has E.J.," he added, shaking his head. "I've worked here for forty years. I've never had anything like this happen before."

Forty *years*? Oh my. This man was like…older than anyone I'd ever met before. Who worked somewhere for forty *years*? What if *I* had to work for forty years…for Kelly! Aaagh!

"Mr. Hanson," I took a deep, steadying breath, trying to refocus on my mission. "Do you know a man named Colin

Williams?"

"Of course," Hanson replied, patting at his swimmy eyes with a napkin. "He was one of the artists on display during the auction."

Of course he was.

"Was he the artist locked in the back room with you?" I asked him.

Hanson shook his head. "It was a new artist. Patrick Patrick. I had only met him once before. Colin has been with us for years."

"Did you say Patrick Patrick?"

"I did."

"Like the same name? First name and last name the same?"

"That's right."

"Um. Right. Is that his real name?"

Hanson stared at me.

"When did you last see him?"

"Colin or Patrick Patrick?"

"Colin."

"It's the strangest thing," Hanson frowned. "He used to come in every week or so but, come to think of it, I haven't seen him in months."

"How many months, exactly?" I asked.

"Oh, let's see," Hanson said slowly. "It must have been around the time of the auction. Yes, I remember. We were auctioning some of his Fifth Series." He pointed to a corner where I assumed Colin's paintings were hung. "He came in with the subject of many of the series' paintings. A woman. They made quite a stunning pair."

I narrowed my eyes. A stunning pair? *A stunning pair!?!* May – when the auction was held – was around the same time Colin proposed to me. This stunning woman better be his mom or grandmother or else.

I thanked the super old man for his time and stomped across the museum to see the stupid subject of this *stunning pair.*

The wall was filled with paintings, about a dozen in all. One was a dark canvas filled with scary floating red boxes and lots of blacks and scariness. It was called "Wistful Thinking," one of Colin's. Another was similar to the ones I'd seen at that first gallery opening I'd crashed – blobs of blues and greens and lameness. The placard beneath it read, "Surreality," by Patrick Patrick. That was the artist who was in the back room with Hanson when the place was getting robbed. I whipped out my notebook and wrote down his name. Then I doodled a big question mark by it. Patrick Patrick. What kind of a stupid ass name is that, anyway?

I glanced at the third painting, a woman sitting in front of a window overlooking the ocean. She was wearing nothing but a thin sheet wrapped around her waist. Her bare back, dotted with vertebra, was hunched slightly. She was looking back over her left shoulder, her right hand barely touching her collarbone. The placard under the painting read "Muse," by Colin Williams.

Leaning in, I took a closer look at the woman's face. Those wide, dark eyes, the mahogany brown hair. My jaw dropped. It was Leah.

Mother fucker.

After I politely thanked old Mr. Hanson for his time (by bursting into tears and running past him), I hightailed it to the bistro he'd mentioned earlier and am now inhaling chocolate croissants and espresso. (Don't judge me. I am on vacation and have just discovered that my lying ex-fiancé is likely a rare diamond ring thief and a two-timer destined for a very scary foreign prison once he turns up again. So I have earned many chocolate croissants and more.)

In summary, my discoverings of the day included the following:

1. My un-special non-diamond engagement ring with an estimated value of $5,000 is now a very special museum-worthy red diamond ring once owned by a rich Italian card player with a fancy sounding name. According to old man Hanson, the estimated value of this museum-worthy ring is $2,200,000. That's two million two hundred thousand dollars. Dollars! The fact that I had been casually wearing something so expensive makes me feel overwhelmed. And anxious. And pissed. But mostly pissed. I'm really trying not to think of all the horrible

things I accidentally did to that ring, like: almost drop it down the sink, almost drop it down the bathtub drain, smash it into the table while talking with my hands and trying to make a point, and, of course, ultimately losing it to ring thieves.

2. My lying assholio of an ex-fiancé was definitely in cahoots with my new but already former friend. My new former friend is back to being an evil, gorgeous, two-timing island bitch. I hate her with a passion and now have to figure out how to get the rest of my stuff out of her mansion without seeing her or talking to her ever again. I'm mega bummed that I'll never get to sleep in her comfy huge guestroom bed anymore or use the massive Jacuzzi tub I saw in her guest bathroom. Lame. So now…

3. I, once again, feel like the bottom of a very used and very smelly trash can. It seems that life both gives and takes away. It is very tough to keep up. Emotionally and otherwise.

Wonderful.

So I guess Leah and Colin were having a muse-ical island affair during or around the same exact time Colin proposed to me with his stolen museum artifact. Who proposes to someone with an expensive stolen museum artifact while engaged in a secret affair with an artistical muse?! I'll tell you who: assholes. Fucking assholes do that. I officially wish I'd never met any of the following people: Leah, Colin, Kelly, my almost-attacker, Colin.

Maybe the true reason for Leah's friendship/free makeover was because she felt bad for sleeping with my fiancé and posing nude in all his paintings. Or maybe she was seriously attempting to get close to me so she could figure out what happened to my ring that drunken night and swoop in to steal it herself without having to pay for it. (This is probably not very likely since she is already a multi-cajillionaire with great looks who has everything, including a very hot boyfriend and a super weekend-only job. What does she want with Colin anyway? Jimmy is way better looking. Quit stealing all my things!)

In any event, the odd reactions I got from Officer Gregory and Leah when I showed them the ring ad now make complete sense.

I do believe I would also react in an odd pissy way if a stupid American tourist flashed an advertisement of a $2.2M stolen ring she claimed was hers. I personally believe that anyone who pranced around town claiming they were in possession of a stolen ring that had been blasted across news and media for months and months was either very stupid or very guilty, or both.

I freaking *hate* Colin for dragging me into a stupid expensive antique jewelry heist that I never had anything to do with in the first place! Grr! He's the sole reason I almost died at the hands of a smelly attacker. He's probably the reason René may or may not have died at the hands of my smelly attacker, and he's also the reason I now have no place to stay and no one to turn to. All my stuff is trapped at Leah's mansion home, including my passport, and I have no way of getting off this dumb island and back home without seeing her again.

Now I know why Colin didn't want to bring me to his secret artist's loft and argued against the St. John honeymoon in the first place. It makes way more sense now. How*ever*, I do think the easier thing would have been to inform me of the fact that he'd proposed with a stolen museum artifact and that going back to the scene of the crime would likely end in kidnapping and/or death for both of us. I would have canceled the trip right away and gone to Peru like Colin had wanted. Obviously. I'd bet no one has even heard of the DeBlume diamond ring or the fancy Italian card player in Peru. We could have honeymooned in peace and done lots of kissing and groping and Jacuzzi tub dipping like newly married people are supposed to.

The sense of urgency around recovering my ring has now dwindled to less than nothing. Even if I did manage to solve the ring stealing mystery like the 007 I am, I'd just have to hand the stupid thing back to Mr. Hanson and his fancy museum since it was never mine to begin with.

I guess I'm back to being a single, penniless, super-loser on her un-honeymoon alone with no friends and no prospects and a stupid dumb job complete with an asshole boss waiting for her back home.

Great.

I'm signing off to start on my third chocolate croissant and drink another espresso and emotionally drown myself in sugar and caffeine. Meanwhile, I'm bracing myself for the next step in my un-honeymoon mission: tracking down Colin's mysterious island loft to see if he has sought refuge there. If he has, I will turn him into the police myself. Then he can rot in a scary foreign prison like he deserves and spend the rest of his days wishing he'd never broken the law and/or had an affair with a gorgeous tropical goddess.

Date: Wednesday
Time: 6:00 p.m.
Location: On island ferry en route to St. John after partially successful St. Thomas trip.
Day Rating (So Far): Remains three stars. However, if my attacker is sighted on St. John, I will immediately reduce the day rating to zero and commence trip-home activities post haste.

Ugh.

I'm definitely feeling the severe after-effects of post-almost-attacking head trauma/subsequent binge drinking episode/emotional breakdown over the $2.2M ring discovery/ensuing chocolate and espresso overload. My head is pounding so hard I can hardly breathe. Plus, sitting on the rocking ferry for like twenty minutes has resulted in a general feeling of unease and major stomach achiness. I haven't even showered yet today and my bangs are becoming very sweaty and pasted-to-forehead like.

I can't even bring myself to think about going back to Leah's mansion to pack up my stuff and flee as fast as I possibly can. If I see her, it will take 100 percent of my strength and effort to avoid what is certain to be a mega-emotional blowout that will include the following topics:

- Fiancé stealing
- Underpants hoarding
- Secret picture taking
- Naked portrait posing

- Possible ring heisting
- Ulterior-motive friendship

I've found myself in a major conundrum. If I do confront Leah with all these new things I know about how horrid and weird she is, I will definitely have to leave her nice mansion and return to my sweaty villa. But I can't return to my sweaty villa because the attacker knows I was staying there and is probably doing a stakeout as we speak and waiting to attack me again as soon as I return.

What should I do? I don't have the funds to rent another place and stay there until my stupid vacation is over on Saturday, and I also don't have the funds to buy an earlier plane ticket home.

The options I'm left with, sadly, are to:

1. Pretend that the underpants-sighting, fiancé-stealing, and pho-to-taking incidents didn't happen so I can continue to sleep in my comfy king bed after taking long luxurious Jacuzzi whirlpool tub baths. (Pro: Can sleep in a comfy king bed after taking long luxurious Jacuzzi whirlpool tub baths. Con: Am currently in a very tenuous emotional state and think keeping my mouth shut is highly unlikely. Especially if I have some more delicious island rum and pharmaceutical medications, which I am definitely planning on having ASAP.)
2. Book another place to stay for the remainder of my un-honeymoon. (Pro: Would solve all problems. Con: Have no money.)
3. Call parents and ask for immediate financial assistance. (Pro: None. Except ability to flee island post haste with dollars in hand. Con: Everyone in Elkton will know that I, twenty-eight year old Sammy Stone, had to call my parents and beg for money so I could cut my island vacation short and return back home with my tail between my legs. Lame.)
4. Track down Shane and both make up with him and then convince him to let me stay with him for the remainder of my un-honeymoon. (Pro: Would be the best life ever. Con: Have no way of contacting Shane and, also, our last meeting went very

badly and ended with mucho yelling and walking away with attitude.)

5. Go back to the sweaty villa and pray no one attacks me and smothers me in my sleep. (Pro: Will not have to be fake-pretend friends with Leah and/or call parents and beg for money. Con: Will likely die at hands of attacker.)

Right.

While I ponder these options and my Ukranian readers thank their lucky stars they aren't me right now, I should probably move on to other news.

So, in other news, I checked the weather report back home from my phone and Elkton is currently getting buried beneath multiple inches of snow while battling blizzard conditions and 17 degree temperatures. Wind chill is currently minus seven. As in seven degrees *below* zero. (Missed calls: 1; Callers: Kelly; Plan: ignore/roll eyes repeatedly; Research: blocking Kelly's phone number.)

On the other hand, St. Thomas/St. John weather is 79 degrees *above* zero and blissfully sunny. The humidity has finally broken, and I am currently trying to work on evolving my spray tan while simultaneously trying not to hurl over the side of the ferry. While I was checking the weather report, I received *yet another* text from my stupid boss Kelly. It read:

Do you not have cell phone capability on St. John? It is my expectation that you call me by end of day. Respond to this message so I am sure you have received. Kelly.

I briefly considered responding with one of the following messages:

- You suck! Your hair is horrible and you wear your pants way too high. Everyone talks about you in the break room and makes fun of your camel tail and laughs at you behind your back. I hate you!

- You are the worst boss of all history and the only reason I will ever speak with you again is to tell you how much I hate you. I hate you!

- I live on the edge. I am a dangerous, attacker-avoiding, ring-mystery detecting super-sleuth with sexy highlights and glowy skin. I take orders from no one! And I hate you!

Sigh.

I decided to respond to Kelly with a professionally appropriate text at the *end* of my un-honeymoon and not one second sooner. Stupid bosses and their stupid extreme expectations! I officially hate all men named Kelly and all other bosses who annoy employees who are on vacation.

In addition, my latest phone check also revealed a picture message from my un-friend Amanda who, in typical un-friend fashion, has taken a picture of the Fleet Farm billboard where her ring advertisement has been replaced by an advertisement for Fleet Farm's new brown cargo work pants. This is Amanda's way of telling me that my ring is no longer better than hers. However, I am very doubtful that her ring was won in a card game by a fancy Italian dude and bestowed upon a probably royal Spanish lady and worth $2.2M. So, in the end, I still win. I wonder if I should respond with a link to a picture of the DeBlume ring before it was stolen by my ex-fiancé. Maybe not.

In summary, despite my makeover and general positivity around my appearance (despite the plastered-to-forehead bang situation), I once again feel that my life is fairly dead-endish and, no matter what, ends with me going back home to my loser life and dire financial situation. Hurrah. *Not.*

Date: Wednesday
Time: 6:15 p.m.

I can't believe I forgot to include an update on my visit to Colin's muse-ical un-artist loft! Turns out, the whole visit was slightly unsettling but hugely uneventful. And, in case you were wondering (spoiler alert!), Colin was nowhere to be found. And his loft wasn't a loft at all. It was some sort of weird mini-house. Anyway...

Recap:
Because I had been reading Colin's mail for quite some time, I actually had the address of his muse-ical loft half-memorized. Well, I remembered the street name at least, so I had no trouble flagging down a cab after my Sapphire Junction visit/croissant and espresso binge episode. I asked the driver to drop me off at Pavilion Street, hoping he knew where that was because I sure didn't. Unfortunately, taking another cab meant I had to part with another fiver. I'm now down to twelve dollars in cash and about the same in fake credit card money.

(By the way, it's super great being a twenty-eight-year-old loser with like twenty dollars to my name and massive credit card debt and a townhouse I can't afford. Not. Staying with a similar aged two-timing un-friend who owns a tropical mansion and expensive books and has great looks and hair makes me feel even better about the whole thing, too. Not. And she owns a Jacuzzi tub and a whole guest wing! And stole my fiancé before he was my fiancé! And probably after he was my fiancé too! I officially hate Leah more than life itself. Stupid un-friends and their hidden agendas. Note to future self: trust no one.)

Anyway, after the cab dropped me off, I spent some time meandering up and down Pavilion Street, realizing that I had, once again, hit an unfortunate dead end. Tiny island house things lined both sides of the street, stacked side-by-side like sardines in a tin can. Each house thing was an exact replica of the last. There was no way to tell them apart except by slight variations in paint color, and I hadn't read Colin's mail close enough to remember what his street number was.

Crap. This was not what I had expected. I'd expected some sort of fancy artist loft with large open spaces and exposed brick. Not a million weird skinny houses all joined together with shared walls and no mailboxes.

I spent some time walking up and down the road like a lost idiot, looking left and right and left again. Every house thing looked the same as the one before. Same size, same shape, same everything. How was I supposed to figure out which was

Colin's? There was no directory to be found, and the one central mailbox didn't have any names listed. It all seemed very suspect and unusual to me.

I reached the end of the road for the hundredth time and stood there, trying to decide what to do. I didn't want to give up so easily and feel like an even bigger loser, but I also didn't particularly feel like going door to door and asking where the former-artist, current-felon Colin Williams lived.

There was a small beach across the street, and I figured I could always hunker down for awhile and do a stakeout type situation. Maybe Colin would show his face eventually. He probably wouldn't. He probably wasn't even on the island at all. I had no idea. I eventually decided that hunkering down would probably be a really bad idea and would probably result in reports to island police about a strange loitering tourist who was really bad at stakeout situations.

I stood at the end of the road like a super dumb and totally alone loser for a few minutes, trying to figure out what to do next. Suddenly, a young island boy on a skateboard flew past me, scaring me into almost having a whack attack. As I glared at him, he skated down the sidewalk, over the curb, and back into the street. The boy glanced at me as he skated by again, taking the same loop as he had before. Aside from the boy and a few tourists who had set up on the beach, the area was scarily quiet.

"Excuse me," I said as the boy neared me a third time. He came to a stop, the scratch of his skateboard echoing down the mostly-deserted street. Hopping off the board, he flipped it up with one foot, grabbing the front end and holding it steady. He seemed very adept with the skateboard for being so young. The boy wore a backwards too-big baseball cap and a baggy t-shirt. He couldn't have been more than eight or nine years old. I suddenly wondered if there were gangs on St. Thomas and, if so, if they recruited boys of about eight or nine on skateboards who wore backwards too-big baseball caps and baggy t-shirts.

"Yeah?" the boy asked, his round brown face dotted with sweat.

"Er –" I said cautiously, watching for him to pull a child-sized gang gun out of his jeans pocket. "I've got a bit of a problem."

No gun appeared from any of the pockets, so I continued.

"I'm looking for an old friend of mine," I said. "And I can't remember which house thing is his."

The boy dropped the end of his board and stepped on it with his right foot, rolling it forward and back.

"I know everyone who lives here," he said proudly. Then he smiled, and I started to feel bad for thinking he might be a gang child.

"You do?" I smiled back. "Well, maybe you can help me then." I tried to sound as friendly and non-stranger-dangerish as possible.

The boy shrugged, eyeing me warily. My non-stranger-danger friendly tone did not seem to be working.

"My friend's name is Colin Williams," I said, sounding desperate. "Do you know him?"

The boy nodded, his eyes locked on mine.

"Do you know where he lives?"

The boy hesitated, the skateboard coming to a stop under his foot.

"I'm Sam," I said, extending my hand out to him. "Samantha, actually, but people call me Sam." (Actually, they call me *Sammy*, but that's super lame and totally over.)

He took my hand gently and gave it a shake. His palm was rough and dry. "I'm Eli," he said quietly.

My heart melted a little over his total cuteness and non-gang-like first name. I'd half-expected something like "Johnny Smalls" or "Tony Two-Face."

"Hi Eli," I said.

I sat down on the curb and patted the ground next to me. Eli flipped the front end of his skateboard up again, grabbed it, and sat down.

"You're pretty good on that skateboard," I told him.

"I practice a lot," he replied. "How come you're looking for Col?"

Hmmm…the former gang child and Colin were on a first name nickname sort of basis. I figured this might be a lucky break. Maybe I could pump this kid for some serious mission info.

"Well," I said. "It's kind of complicated."

"That's okay," Eli said. "I'm pretty grown up for my age."

I chuckled and whipped out my cell phone, flipping through a couple pictures of Colin and me.

"How come you're not in school?" I asked after Eli peeked at the pictures.

"I'm skipping," Eli said. "I hate school."

"I hated school too," I said. "But you still have to go."

Eli sighed, hopping up and jumping back on his skateboard. "That's what Col used to say."

"Were you good friends?" I asked.

Eli nodded. "He was my only grown up friend," he said sadly.

Was? Interesting...

Eli continued. "We used to hang out after school sometimes and play video games, talk about stuff. He was teaching me the guitar." The boy stared off into the distance, eyes squinting in the sun. He shrugged. "Then he was just gone."

"Do you know where he went?" I asked.

Eli shook his head. "He didn't even say goodbye or nothing."

"Anything," I said automatically.

Eli gave me a sheepish smile. "That's what Col used to say."

A battered brown Jeep turned down Pavilion Street and headed our way.

"Oh man," Eli said. "That's my mom, I gotta go."

He scraped his toe against the pavement and headed for one of the tick-a-tack house things to our left. Turning back to me, he grinned. "Colin lives there, or used to," he said, pointing to a house thing in the middle of the row on the opposite side of the street. "If you see him, can you tell him thanks for me?"

"Thanks for what?" I asked, standing up and brushing off my bottom.

"For the picture. He left it in my bedroom, next to his hat," he said, pointing to his backwards cap. He started to skate away but slowed to look over his shoulder. "And for everything else," he shouted.

The Jeep came to a stop along the sidewalk and Eli hopped off his skateboard. As he ran to open the door for his mother, I found my faith in children restored. Sort of.

A young woman climbed out, giving me an odd 'what are you doing talking to my son, you strange American' sort of look. I gave her a thin, hopefully non-creepy smile in response and began walking toward Colin's house thing, leaving her and Eli behind.

So there I was, standing in the middle of the street, about to visit the secret getaway of my soon-to-be imprisoned, two-timing ex-fiancé.

I suddenly wished I'd done at least one of the following to prepare for my potential-ex-fiancé-reunion: showered, fixed my makeup, fixed my hair (especially my bangs), put on better clothes, brushed my teeth, went on a diet.

It had only been like four days since I'd seen Colin, but it felt like four years. Would he even recognize me with my new highlights and bangs? I didn't think so.

As I stood in front of his door, I started feeling panicky and gross. Even though I knew he probably wouldn't be home, I couldn't help but wonder what would happen if he were home. I found myself wishing that he would both be there and not be there, even though I knew that would defy all the laws of physics and result in a complete emotional/mental breakdown on my part. I decided to pop a half-Xanax to make it through and tried not to think of my two-hour post-almost-attack therapy call and the therapist urging me to confront my possible Xanax addiction. It was only an addiction if you admitted it out loud, right? Plus, it wasn't like Dr. Brad would keep prescribing them to me if he thought I was addicted to them. Right? Plus, it was only a half one. I could have taken a whole one. So there.

Anyway, I walked up the two steps to Colin's front door, pushed a small doorbell, and heard the high tinkle of a bell echoing inside. I listened for footsteps through the door and rapped my knuckles loudly against the doorframe. Nothing.

Unfortunately, I hadn't had the forethought to formulate a successful back-up plan in the event Colin really wasn't home. Standing there staring at his door, I eventually decided that my only option, given the limited un-honeymoon time I had left, was to break in.

That's right. I was going to break in to my former fiancé's secret muse-ical island house thing. The place where he most likely painted and then banged the brains out of my former friend/free makeover-giver.

I had never broken into any place before, especially since I never ended up having to break into the sweaty villa, and I was feeling a bit anxious about the whole thing. In the end, I figured that, since Colin and I were supposed to be married a few days ago, half-technically the house thing was half-mine anyway. Breaking in would simply be a way to gain access to my half.

Of course, I lacked the first idea as to what a successful break-in process entailed. Sleuths in movies always used bobby pins or tiny knife devices to poke around in the lock a bit until a certain noise happened and the door popped open, but I didn't have a bobby pin or tiny knife device. Busting in through a window was also a non-option – it was the middle of the day and someone would report me for sure. Plus I'd bloody my knuckles. Explaining my attacker-induced bloodied knees to my parents and boss was already going to be hard enough. Trying to explain bloodied knees *and* knuckles? I'd send my parents spiraling into a series of massive strokes and heart attacks.

Another Jeep – a shimmery fire engine red – turned down the road. Its tires squealed as it rounded the corner and the sound threw off my pre-break-in analysis. I searched around for a spare key, a bobby pin, or a tiny knife device, but there was nothing but gravel and patches of sad grassy sand. I realized I was just standing on the front stoop of my ex-fiancé's crappy mini-house, thinking about how to break in and starting to look highly obvious.

As the Jeep came closer, I grew even more panicky and sweaty and became certain that the person driving the Jeep was the police officer I'd pissed off, the attacker, or Colin himself.

Crap.

All I could think to do was to grab the doorknob, squeeze my eyes shut, and chant, "Please, please work! Please, oh please!"

The knob turned easily in my hand.

Then the door opened, and I fell inside before the Jeep passed me.

I took this as evidence that the curse on me had finally been broken. Things were finally going my way for the first time ever. Hurrah!

I quickly shut the door behind me and, just like that, I was safely inside Colin's old shitty mini-house. It smelled like rotten garbage and sour everything, and it wasn't too tough to tell that the place had been completely and utterly ransacked. In fact, the reason the doorknob turned so easily in my hand was because someone had already broken in. The security chain was lying in a pile on the ground, snapped in two. My 007 instincts kicked in when I realized that the broken chain meant that someone, likely Colin, was inside when the break-in happened. Or that he had chained the door and gone out the back or something.

I walked through the main entry, shards of glass crunching under my sandals. A couch, two side tables, a coffee table, and a chair all lay overturned in the living room. Paintings had been ripped from the walls and thrown to the ground, some slashed from corner to corner. The television screen was smashed, and shards of what used to be a ceramic vase were scattered underneath the TV.

For a half-second, I almost felt bad for Colin. I mean, someone had trashed all his stuff! That's just horrible. Then I remembered how horrible *he* was at life and at being a decent human being and how he'd gotten his own self into this mess by making a series of very bad decisions put together. Then, because ruining his own life wasn't enough, he decided to put me right in the middle of it. He practically implicated me the second he slid that billion dollar ring on my finger and told me some lame story about how it was some stupid garnet and one-of-a-kind and blah blah et cetera. Then he put my life in the worst danger ever when he agreed to a honeymoon on the same freaking tropical island chain as the gallery he'd just been party to robbing. Thanks a lot. Jerk.

Sure, my time on the island had been emotionally confusing in both a positive and negative way and, sure, I had an awesome new look and a semi-new outlook on life after nearly dying at the hands of a ring-wanting-sausage-armed henchman. Sure, I'd started to come out of my cocoon a little bit and was starting to become a confident butterfly/super-sleuth and, yeah, I had even gotten a little excited about the whole ring mission thing. But, despite it all, Colin could have at least told me the truth. He should have trusted me, of all people, since he was about to marry me like five seconds ago. Although I suppose he trusted Leah and told her everything instead after he painted her naked and then banged her brains out right under my nose.

Fucking lame.

Anyway, Colin had obviously ditched his nasty trashed skinny house quite some time ago because the whole smelly, dusty place seemed like it had been empty for awhile.

As much as I hated to admit it, I was a little bummed about the apparent non-reunion situation. I'd been looking forward to the yelling and throwing things and learning the truth about why he gave me the DeBlume ring in the first place. And showing off my new look and making him feel sorry for dumping me last minute and leaving me for dead and painting Leah naked in his stupid pictures instead.

Every inch of the place had been completely destroyed. The ransackers even overturned the contents of Colin's fridge; the kitchen floor was littered with puddles of ketchup and relish and sticky milk. Like anyone would hide a $2.2M ring in a carton of milk, I scoffed. Get real. The trash bin was overflowing with crap and the only thing remaining in Colin's fridge was a half bottle of Chardonnay and a crusty wedge of moldy Swiss cheese. I nearly poured myself a glass of the Chardonnay but talked myself out of it so I could keep my wits and things about me. Then I congratulated myself for having such great willpower.

After digging through the kitchen and finding nothing of interest except ants and creepy centipedes and things, I fled up the stairs where the smell didn't make me feel so queasified.

The first room off the stairs was Colin's studio. A large bay window spanned one wall and offered a partial ocean view, although only the tiniest sliver of blue water was visible (and only if you smooshed your face really close to the glass). I didn't see what was so muse-ical about that. The window was open and a soft breeze filtered in. Dozens of paintings filled the room. They were stacked edge to edge on the floor, lining the walls from corner to corner. Some stacks were three or four paintings deep. They'd been rifled through, tossed around, and discarded. Some were lying face down on the wood floor. One was trapped under the overturned easel, another lying amongst a handful of paint-brushes and rags.

Although I wanted to, I refused to look at any of the paintings. I had no desire to see Leah looking all naked and wide-eyed again. Instead, I left the studio and found Colin's bedroom, where he likely had lots of two-timing sex with his naked, wide-eyed fiancé stealer. I was starting to feel like I was in one of those Lifetime movies where the main woman finds out that her husband has two completely different families and she walks through the other woman's house and looks at all her stuff and then murders her.

The whole thing felt horribly wrong and illegal. Colin never wanted me to see this place and then, there I was, walking through it after it had been trashed and abandoned, wondering where he was and if he was even alive anymore. Funny how things just change like that.

The bedroom had been upended like the rest of the house. Clothes I'd never seen before covered everything. I moved a few shirts to make a spot for myself on the bed, sat down, and dug my cell phone out of my purse. I ignored *another* missed call from Kelly (no text this time), and opened my contact list. My fingers started to shake.

It was time.

It had been a couple days since I'd tried calling Colin. He didn't answer on our wedding day, of course, when I'd called him a billion times and left at least a hundred messages on his voicemail – ranging from politely concerned to furious to a sob-bing, emotionally destroyed mess.

I really didn't want to call him while sitting on his bed in his smelly ripped-apart mini-house, but I had to. I had to talk to him. I had to see if he would answer. I had to ask him why he gave me the ring. Why he brought me into the middle of a highly illegal situation. If he ever loved me at all or if it was all just a game. Okay, maybe I didn't want the answer to those questions. Just the first one.

I took a deep breath and pressed his number before I could talk myself out of it. I held the phone to my ear, my heart thumping against my ribcage. I honestly couldn't decide if I wanted him to answer or not but, eventually, I figured I had to at least know if he was still alive.

I shouldn't have been so concerned.

After a few seconds of static, a message clicked on and a woman's voice told me that Colin's number had been disconnected. Then she asked me to hang up and try my call again.

So I did.

After listening to the message a second time, I turned my phone off and slid it back into my purse.

He'd had his number disconnected.

I promptly burst into tears and cried all over my lap and the clothes pile. Then I grabbed a t-shirt that still smelled like him and buried my face into it and sobbed some more.

What had happened to us? Who was this person I had been ready to commit my whole life to? I thought I knew him. I thought he loved me. Obviously I was wrong. I didn't know him at all. And he didn't love me at all. Stupid a-hole.

Still, I couldn't help but wonder if there was a deeper meaning behind his wedding no-show. What if he'd been attacked by the same sausage-armed asshole who'd attempted to attack me? What if he was dead? Even so, a phone call would have been nice. He'd texted his friend Billy, after all, to tell Billy he wasn't coming to the wedding. He could have texted me, too. Unless it was the attacker who texted Billy. From Colin's phone!

(Okay, I'll admit that my theories were getting a little crazy, even for me.)

I pulled myself back together and popped another half-Xanax. (It's only an addiction if you admit it out loud.) I wiped my nose and eyes on Colin's t-shirt and tossed it back into the clothes pile. As I was leaving the bedroom, something reflected in the mirror across the hall and caught my eye.

I went back into the room and saw a picture frame sitting on top of Colin's dresser. Because I was a bona fide 007 and didn't want to leave fingerprints on anything, I scooped up two hopefully clean socks that were lying on the floor and slid my hands into them like gloves. The picture frame was heavy and disgustingly gaudy. It was silver and lined with mismatched fake plastic gemstones that were glued onto the frame. I rubbed at one of the gemstones with my hand sock and it popped off, falling onto the ground and bouncing under the bed. Whoops.

Inside the frame was a picture of Colin and Eli, the little boy on the skateboard I'd met outside. Their faces were pressed together cheek-to-cheek. Eli's grin couldn't have been any bigger. Colin looked sunburned and windswept and heart achingly gorgeous. I ran my fingers over the multicolor gemstones, remembering a similar frame I had at home; it was a birthday gift from my seven-year-old niece, who lived a few houses down from my parents. Another gemstone popped off and bounced on the bed. Before I knew what I was doing, I'd popped them all off. I shouldn't have done that. I don't know why I did. Except it felt so good.

I grimaced, setting the ruined frame back on the dresser and leaving the room. I'd never seen Colin look so happy before. Stupid. He hadn't even told me he had a little friend on the island. Then again, I guess he hadn't told me a lot of things.

I poked around the house a bit more before I left but didn't find anything interesting. Aside from the picture of Colin and Eli, there was nothing personal in the house at all. No other pictures, no notebooks or journals, no books. The bathroom was empty, too. No shampoo, razor, toothbrush or toothpaste, no deodorant. Nothing.

Maybe Colin had somehow managed to escape before the house-trashers busted in. Maybe he grabbed his man-products and fled out the back door like I'd initially thought. Maybe he was still alive and not kidnapped at all. Maybe he was the one who stole the ring off my finger when I was drunk and then sold it for cajillions of dollars and was now living on a beach in Tahiti laughing at me and all my super dumbness.

Dick.

I'd been in the house for at least an hour and desperately needed a break from the spoiled garbage smells and total nastiness. If there were any clues to be had, the ransackers had probably gotten to them long before I did. I peeked outside before I opened the front door to make sure there were no colorful Jeeps or random people around waiting to grab me and ask me why I was loitering and talking with small children and then breaking into skinny houses. Then, keeping the sock-gloves on, I opened the door and quickly stepped out, rubbing the doorknob and doorbell before removing the socks and sticking them in my purse.

Aside from any potential DNA evidence in the tears/sob snot I'd left all over Colin's t-shirt, I felt pretty good about my first break-in. I mean, technically I should have grabbed the t-shirt as well, but I really didn't want to go back in there. I was already emotionally empty and starting to get very tired and thirsty.

In conclusion, I didn't really uncover any additional clues during my visit, aside from knowing that, probably, whoever wanted the ring knew Colin and knew where he lived. And that Colin disconnected his damn phone number and was secret friends with a neighbor kid. None of this was very helpful evidence on the whole.

Except...the whole thing made me wonder. If Colin stole the ring and gave it to me, why would someone trash his apartment? Why wouldn't they spend all their time coming after me? Did Colin steal the ring from the gallery and then disappear, causing the ring-wanter to trash his place in hopes of finding clues? Or did someone else steal the ring and, if so, how did Colin come across it? If Colin did come across it, why did he steal it from the stealer in the first place? And, again, why the hell did he give it to me?

Just thinking about it makes my head throb.

Anyway, the ferry is docking at Cruz Bay now. The sun is setting and bugs are starting to gnaw at my thighs, so I am off to return to Leah's mansion and either confront her about her two-timing evil bitchiness/underpants-stealing *or* drink heavily and pass out on the comfy king-sized bed after taking an epically long Jacuzzi whirlpool bath and watching *Love Actually* for the billionth time.

I mean, it's not like I actually *want* to go back to Leah's place. Technically I hate her. But the alternate options of either calling my parents or returning to my attacker-infested sweaty villa are just too scary to even think about.

Tomorrow, I will dedicate all my time to (1) finding Shane, (2) returning his suspicious wallet, (3) showing him my new hot look, and (4) pursuing a sexual escapade. Then I will solve my mission and go home in peace. I feel so close, yet so far away.

Until next time…

Comment from Kristy K.: Hello Sam! My name is Kristy and I am from Chenobiquon, Wisconsin! We live just a few hours from each other! I came across your blog diary on Reddit when I was bored at work today and read all your posts. Did you know that you have 7 followers on Reddit? You have a few thumbs up and a few thumbs down, but mainly thumbs up. I'm going to give you a thumbs up, I think. Is your story for real? Were you actually almost attacked? Did Leah actually steal your underpants? Why would she do that? ~ Kristy

Comment from Sam: Hi Kristy, Sam here. I am familiar with Chenobiquon. I went there once about twenty years ago to compete in a spelling bee. I lost on the last word, even though I knew how to spell the word. I was afraid of winning back then, but I'm not anymore (I have bangs now). Seven followers, wow. Do people actually read blog diaries, do you think? Aside from when they're bored at work? Yes, the story is for real. I don't know why Leah took the underpants, but I will let you know if I find out. Thanks for not being an Internet solicitor or a Ukrainian bride.

Comment from Anonymous: she could in up in a bind he did not foresee to assuming everything is O.K. from start

Comment from Sam: What?

Comment from rednOsHold: I got flat stomach in 4 weeks learn how you can to. <scary Internet link>

Comment from Sam: GET OFF MY BLOG GODDAMMIT!

Date: Wednesday
Time: 8:00 p.m.
Location: Leah's mansion.

Day Rating (So Far): Eh.

So I officially have more than zero blog diary readers, which is amazing seeing as I didn't even do anything to try and get more readers. I feel so very loved and interesting! I'm currently entertaining dreams of becoming a full-time blog diary writer, moving to New York City, buying a pair of fancy shoes, and purchasing a closet-sized apartment overlooking Central Park. Perhaps I can compile my blog diary posts into a hardcover blog diary coffee table book that avid readers will purchase and read and love like in *Sex and the City*. Then I can quit my dumb job, get out of dumb Elkton, and enjoy a non-traditional writer's life where I make my own hours and am my own boss.

Great plan!

Knowing that I have more than zero blog diary readers and that one of my blog diary readers lives in Wisconsin makes me feel a little anxious. I mean, who else might stumble upon my blog diary? What if it's someone I know? Worse yet, what if it's someone who knows me? Thankfully, pretty much everyone I know lives in Elkton and pretty much no one in Elkton really knows how to use the Internet – except for me, my un-friend Melody, and Martha Shaker, our librarian. I think my blog diary is safe, for now.

After the ferry ride back to St. John, I decided that my only real next-step option was to return to Leah's tropical mansion and either confront or avoid her for the rest of my trip. Since I had neither the courage nor the inclination to return to the sweaty, attacker-friendly villa or call my parents, my only other options were really not options at all.

Fortunately, upon arriving at the mansion, I discovered that Leah was out for the night. Yay! All my problems were solved until morning!

Leah had left a yellow post-it note on the granite kitchen countertop that read:

Out with Jimmy. Don't wait up. Food in fridge and movies in funny cupboard (the one in the living room with the post-it on it). See you tomorrow. Xo. Leah.

Hurrah! I had the whole entire mansion to myself for the whole night and didn't have to worry about confronting Leah and her two-timing, panty-stealing ways until tomorrow.

And yes, she did actually write me an 'Xo' in her note like we were best friends or something when, in reality, she had stolen my ex-fiancé before he was my *ex*-fiancé *and* took voyeuristic photos of me when I wasn't looking! What a dick.

Just for that, I decided to use her Jacuzzi whirlpool tub and all her expensive bubble bath.

Two blissful hours later...

The Jacuzzi whirlpool tub and loads of expensive bubble bath proved to be life-alteringly delicious and soul-soothing. I used the soaking time to think more about the ring mystery in a valiant-yet-useless attempt to ponder each of my disparate ring clues while also figuring out where Colin was hiding. I also risked iPad drowning to do some Googling regarding the DeBlume diamond and other related things.

I'm proud to report that the review of my detecting notebook and un-honeymoon memory bank resulted in a successful ability to patch a small series of clues together and obtain another clue!

In true mission-sensitive 007 fashion, I did some Internet digging into the owner of the sweaty villa. I wanted to know which mysterious friend gave Colin such a great discount on the crusty nasty place. Then I would confront that friend, do some aggressive interrogations, and demand that he give up all Colin-related information without delay.

In no time at all, I discovered that the mysterious villa-owning friend was none other than Miss Leah V. de Medici, our favorite underpants-stealing mistress. Aaagh! Does she own everything?? (PS - I had no idea she had such a fancy last name. I'm convinced she's the lucky recipient of a multi-cajillion dollar fancy-last-name inheritance. Lame.)

I am now approximately 100 percent certain that Colin is hiding out somewhere in Leah's sweaty villa. Why? Probably (1) because Colin and Leah are secret artist lovers and (2) because Colin is also hiding from scary attackers, as am I, and is concurrently trying to avoid going to prison.

I remembered the nasty fridge leftovers I'd found in the villa when I first arrived *and* the dirty dishes in the sink *and* the weird sleeping bag situation in the dirty under-villa area I'd noticed when searching for a way to break in after being almost-attacked. Colin was *definitely* living there. I couldn't believe I didn't see it right away. He was probably there while *I* was there. That stupid dick! I guess I should have been way better at my deductive logics in the first place instead of distracted by island happy hours and the no hot water situation. (Note to future self: get way better at deductive logics, read all the Sherlock Holmes and Nancy Drews and take notes on all their deductive logics, practice all the logics.)

Sure, it could be a long shot. It could just be a homeless person or one of the construction people from next door, but it was definitely worth investigating. Especially since Colin knew I would be staying in the villa for the whole week and probably thought it would be the last place I would come looking for him.

He was almost right. Almost. He forgot how smart and awesomely great I am at deducing and things.

After my Jacuzzi experience and successful sleuthing operation, I grabbed some leftover mac & cheese from Leah's fridge and gobbled it down while checking out her funny cupboard out of sheer curiosity. I'm not quite sure why she calls it a funny cupboard. It looked like a regular old cupboard to me. It was filled with like 1,000 DVDs and, randomly, with tons of shoes and purses and accessories. (I may or may not have borrowed a pair of expensive designer sunglasses and an expensive designer purse for my potential reunion with Colin. I obviously want to look awesome before all the ass-kicking starts. Sure it's like eight o'clock at night and I don't need the sunglasses, but they're going to look super great sitting atop my head behind my bangs.)

I'm signing off to go search the sweaty villa from top to bottom. I hope to God I don't encounter any more attackers. I also hope to God I'll uncover Colin and force him to tell me everything he knows about the ring and everything that happened with Leah, his stupid naked muse lady. This will help me solve the mission and return the ring to old Mr. Hanson and help him restore his faith in humanity and things. Hurrah! I feel so very confident and mission-successful. Believe I am better at missions than 007 himself.

Date: Thursday
Time: 5:00 a.m.
Location: Leah's mansion's king-sized guest bed. With, miraculously, a very sexy island god in bed next to me!! Allow me to repeat: WITH A VERY SEXY ISLAND GOD IN BED NEXT TO ME!!!
Day Rating (So Far): Infinity!

Shhh...

I must be very quiet. I can't even begin to describe how incredible and amazing the last nine hours have been. I have not slept one wink but, instead, waited for my gorgeous bed-mate to fall asleep before ripping out my iPad for an incredible blog diary update.

Recap:
Last night, I shut down my iPad and emotionally braced myself for the drive back to my sweaty villa. I was thoroughly prepared to conduct a full investigation of the villa and the under-villa area and, once I found Colin or the homeless person who was living there, probably yell and scream and kick lots of things. Then, the most wondrous event happened.
It all began with a knock at the door.

I had just finished blow-drying my bangs, wrestling my hair into a not-so-chic-but-getting-chicer bun, and unsuccessfully attempting to apply and blend eye shadow for the first time ever. With a semi-fashionable cobalt blue sundress and Leah's designer sunglasses and purse, I felt very glamorous and positive and ready to see Colin again.

The knock at the door irritated me at first because I assumed it would be someone I didn't know or want to talk to. Probably someone who was looking for Leah. This annoying person would waste time asking lots of bothersome questions, and I would have to explain where Leah was without letting any negative comments regarding her horrible friendship slip through. Since I was very busy and important with freshly washed hair and goodish makeup, I really didn't want to do all that. However, I answered anyway because I had parked my Jeep outside and was too anxious to try and hide while the door-knocker went around and looked into all the windows and saw me standing around trying to avoid opening the door.

I whipped the door open with irritation in my heart only to see my tropical island, on-again/off-again, emotionally-complex-but-so-incredibly-sexy-I-don't-even-care vacation sex god standing in front of me. Hurrah!

Shane was wearing dark blue jeans, a dark gray polo, and a backwards baseball cap. He looked so deliciously good I nearly orgasmed just standing there drooling on him. It took him a second to realize it was me standing there and not Leah. When he did, he looked very startled and highly relieved.

"Sam!" he exclaimed, rushing in and wrapping me up in his arms. (See what I mean about the emotional complexity?)

"Oh Sam, I'm so sorry. I'm so sorry. I'm so glad you're okay." He held me for a very long time and it felt very good and lower-belly warming. (I may or may not have dusted off the mental penis image and held it in my mind during the entirety of the hugging. It was coming in useful for so many different things already!)

I didn't even really care about Shane's sudden change in demeanor. Sure, he was strangely bipolar and emotionally confused about everything. He liked me then he didn't, he found my travel bag at the airport and shared a cab with me only to ditch me on the ferry, then he disappeared into thin air, then he reappeared and bought me loads of Cherry Bombs only to disappear again, then he reappeared and bought me some wine and fish

Shane – I mean Edward – laughed. "Eddie is fine," he said. "Some people call me Jacobs."

"Jacobs? I will absolutely not be calling you Jacobs. That's the stupidest nickname I've ever heard of."

Eddie laughed again. "Just Eddie, then." He frowned. "You're taking this surprisingly well."

"Well," I said, ignoring the fact that my heart was pumping at like 1,000 beats per minute and I was stress sweating through my sundress. "Since I've stepped foot on this island, I've been robbed, almost-attacked, and hit by a bath – never mind."

I gave him a wan smile, my eyes going swimmy. I didn't really know what to think – him being a writer and then not being a writer, then being a special agent with a different name. It was all a lot to take in. But, I was at least a billion times more attracted to him now that he was so top-secret and important.

"I'm so sorry, Sam," Sha– no, Eddie said. "I was supposed to look after you."

I have something you can look after, I thought to myself. It's in my underpants. My cheeks went red. I tried to think about anything else.

"You're investigating the DeBlume, then?" I asked, changing the subject. Eddie looked surprised. "I figured it out," I explained.

"You did?" said Shane. I mean Eddie. (This whole name change thing is very hard to get used to.) "I'm impressed," he said. "Really."

"Let your boss know about that," I said. "Tell him I figured it all out by myself."

(Hurrah! I've collected the same evidence as the CIA! I mean the FBI! (Same difference.) I am *definitely* on my way to becoming an official 007 mission-contributor.)

"I will," Eddie said with a smile.

God, he was so sexy.

New Plan:

1. Learn everything about what Eddie knows about the diamond situation and

2. Proceed to jump on him and drag him into my king-sized bed and epically hump him all night long.

Turns out, Eddie had been on St. John for nearly five months. He came after the DeBlume Red, my un-engagement ring, was stolen last May. He's been "Undercover Shane" ever since. His trail ran cold weeks ago and his boss finally called him back home to Washington D.C. He was waiting for his plane to arrive when he saw me deboarding my plane. He recognized the ring straight away.

At first, he thought I was the ring thief but figured out that I wasn't when he learned that I actually had no clue what the ring was in the first place or what it was worth. And that I was a dumb Midwesterner who didn't know anything about anything. And that I had never been on a plane before. And that I was wearing the ring in public and showing the ring ad to everyone like a super dumb idiot. And lots of other things.

"So…what gave it away?" I asked innocently after he'd finished telling me all about how he figured out that I wasn't the ring thief.

"What didn't give it away?" Eddie responded with a smile.

Right.

We had gaffed a bottle of Leah's wine and opened it with enthusiasm. Eddie had turned on the electric fire and flipped on one of Leah's romantic CDs. The whole night was beginning to turn very romantic and was becoming filled with so many romantic possibilities. I'd forgotten all about Colin and the villa-investigating excursion because, obviously, this was way infinity better than that would have been.

"Did you steal it?" I asked.

"What?"

"Are you the one who stole my ring on Sunday night, when I was drunk and un-salsa dancing with you?"

"Guess again," he smiled, draining his wine glass and refilling both of our glasses. God, he was so sexy. I wanted to crawl into his lap and die.

"The kid from the beach?" I shook my bangs at him. "The one who interrupted our…"

I gasped. It all came back to me in one wild rush. The black curtains that had blocked out my memory momentarily parted, ter? Our sexual oceanic episode? Our lap grindage and romantic ear whisperings followed by my subsequent emotional outburst? I settled with, "After I last saw you. I went to St. Thomas on Wednesday morning."

"But –"

"How did you think I knew about the DeBlume?" I asked.

"Er –" Eddie became flustered, his cheeks going red. "I thought Leah might have told you," he said finally. "It's just – I thought...You never came back to the villa. I thought you were..." He trailed off.

What was the big deal? It's not like he was my dad or anything. It felt kind of creepy knowing I had a special FBI agent man keeping an eye on me. I wondered if he'd seen me do anything awful, like pull my thong out of my butt crack or lean forward to reposition my boobs in my bra. I doubted he would be touching knees and drinking wine with me if he had.

"Well I went," I said. "And the manager guy told me everything." I gestured for more wine. "He showed me pictures of the diamond and told me all about the robbery and the cameras and everything."

Eddie looked surprised and I felt very confident and amazing. "How did you manage that?" he asked.

"I might have led him to think I was a private detective."

"What?" Eddie coughed, sputtering. "Sam, you can't do stuff like that. You need a special license and..."

"I know, I know. But it worked," I waved him off, shaking my bangs. "I know pretty much everything you do now."

Eddie smiled. "I doubt that very much," he said.

Another half-bottle of wine later, I was feeling very tipsy and sensual. Eddie was getting good at doing sexy things like brushing my cheek with his finger and kissing my forehead when I least expected it, and I was getting good at sexy chuckling and touching his bicep every few minutes. Or seconds, whatever.

Now that Eddie had blown his cover with me (and everyone who reads this blog diary), he finally told me all about his life in D.C. He was single, lived in a shitty townhouse in Arlington, Virginia, ate Thai takeout most nights, and had a two-disc subscription to Netflix. He used to have a peace lily plant for something to take care of but, seeing as he'd been on St. John for five months, he thinks it probably went dry some time ago.

I, in turn, told him all about Elkton and the pretzel court and my job and how Colin had stood me up on my wedding day.

"Do you think he might have been kidnapped or…or hurt?" I asked Eddie quietly. It had been on my mind constantly since I left Colin's ransacked, abandoned house thing.

I wanted to believe that Leah was secretly harboring him and that it was his takeout sushi bag I'd seen in the fridge of the sweaty villa, but it was impossible to know for sure. If the guy who'd tried to attack me was also after him…my stomach turned. What if he was dead? What if my Colin, my sweet floppy-haired artist, was gone? All because I wanted to come to St. John instead of Peru. Tears pricked my eyes.

"Sam," Eddie was shaking me gently, snapping me back. "Are you alright? Do you need some water?"

I nodded. While he was in the kitchen, I blinked back my swimmy tears and pulled myself together. Why was I even upset? What Colin and I had was done. Over. He'd lied to me and ruined my life and financial freedom and made very, very bad decisions about painting naked people and giving people stolen rings. Nothing could ever make me want to get back together with him. Period.

Plus, now I had a sexy FBI special agent, who was getting me a glass of water and doing lots of other great things. Me. Sam Stone from Elkton, Minnesota, a.k.a. the Armpit of the Midwest. I was sitting on a leather couch in front of an electric fire, having just taken a luxurious Jacuzzi whirlpool bath and eaten lots of gourmet mac & cheese. I was enjoying several glasses of spendy wine and was about to drag a gorgeous chiseled man into a very large, very comfortable bed. It was all so very romantic and exciting, and I congratulated myself for having such a cool life and not taking any Xanax along with my wine for the first time all week. I was on the verge of becoming seriously spoiled by all the lavish, tropical, non-job living and furiously tried not to think about having to leave my sexy FBI agent and go back home to the cold and the snow and the meat plant in a few short days. At this point, death by attacker seemed like a much better alternative.

Eddie came back with the glass of water and sat down. I took it as an opportunity to jump on him and shove my face toward his right away. I'm happy to report that it worked like a dream. We commenced a thoroughly blissful heavy make out session, during which Eddie did a very sexy lower-lip-nibble maneuver that was totally heavenly and made me forget about Colin once and for all. Almost.

Then Eddie picked me up like I was a genuine Princess Bride and carried me elegantly into the guest room. I felt so very elegant and woozy and swooned appropriately, trying not to faint while simultaneously ripping off his baseball cap and polo shirt and finally rubbing my hands all over his naked abs. It was a Christmas miracle! A dream come true! It was everything I thought it could be.

By the time Eddie slipped off my sundress, my body was trembling so badly he stopped and asked if I was alright.

"Yes," I murmured between kisses. "Oh yes."

There were so many kisses, I can't even begin to describe all of them. They started at my toes and trailed up my calves, my shins, my thighs. Between my thighs. Deliciously tender. Below my belly button, winding across my rib cage, across each breast, up my neck and, finally, landing on my lips.

Because this is blog diary is rated PG-13 due to strong language and partial nudity, I will skip all the NC-17 rated details – like when I wrapped my fingers around Eddie's hot, thick penis of earlier and nearly orgasmed at the hotness and the thickness of it, or when he traced my lower lip with his index finger, pushed it past my lips into my mouth and, after I wetted it with my tongue, inserted it somewhere else, somewhere that had never been treated so nicely before by any man, anywhere, at any time.

(Confession: Usually, when I have sex with a guy for the first time, I fake my orgasm. This makes the guy feel good and like he's doing something relatively successful down there and, as a result, I feel good too, albeit slightly under-fulfilled. But with Eddie, it was different. I nearly real orgasmed just looking at his face and abs and, when his fingers were inside me, I real orgasmed for real. And again when he was inside me – the whole of him, hot and hard – and I didn't even have to fantasize about my Thunder From Down Under calendar or anything.)

By the time all was said and done, I'd real orgasmed twice and felt that my whole life had been leading up to this particular moment. I was very on top of the world. I had fire in my bones and was sexually fulfilled for the first time in my life. (Sorry Colin.) Eddie really *was* a tropical sex god. A good one. And a secret agent too! And I'd slept with him! Me, Sam Stone. Of the large forehead, plain-ish features, awkward personality variety. It was all so wonderful and unusual. I never wanted the moment to end. So we had sex again. And then he fell asleep.

Now he's sleeping, and I'm trying not to sleep so I can soak up every single second I have left of my un-honeymoon and hopefully have sex at least a hundred million more times before I have to go back home to Elkton.

I never, ever want this vacation to end. Never!

I'm signing off now to spoon and cuddle and drool all over the place. I'm also going to try to snap a photo of Eddie to prove that I actually bedded a chiseled, GQ worthy, bona fide 007. Great plan!

Date: Thursday
Time: 10:00 a.m.
Location: Leah's mansion.
Day Rating (So Far): Horrible. Worse than horrible. Am wallowing in very intense feelings of post-sex inadequacy.

I wish I could say that Eddie and I enjoyed a very nice post-marathon nap with a subsequent romantic lie-in complete with breakfast in bed and lots more sex, but I accidentally drifted off to sleep after spooning and cuddling with his sleeping naked body. When I woke up, he was gone.

No note, no phone number, no message, no nothing. Just gone.

Aaaagh!

I feel decrepit and disgustingly under-skilled as a romantic lover. I truly believe that, if Eddie enjoyed the sex as much as I did, he would have stuck around until I woke up so he could get more of the sex. Right?

I have a feeling I'll find out later that he's either a liar, a pig, or dating Leah. That would be just my luck. Stupid curse.

Speaking of, the ring stealing, fiancé stealing Leah is still not back from her overnight date with Jimmy the sexy bartender, so the entire mansion is completely empty and horribly empty feeling. All the empty feelings, paired with Eddie's post-sex abandonment and my rapidly dwindling vacation time, made me feel like one lonely, horribly depressed loser. With great eyebrows. And bangs. But horribly depressed nonetheless.

To combat the evil feelings, I've decided that, after a huge breakfast of eggs and bacon and potatoes out on the terrace, I am going to continue where I left off yesterday before being so rudely (but wonderfully) interrupted by Eddie and his writer-not-writer-Shane-not-Shane-FBI-agent-undercover mysteriousness. (And yes, just so you know, Leah's mansion walks out to a terrace which walks out to the beach which walks out to the ocean. I hate her and wish she would die and bequeath her mansion to me in her will, along with free spa treatments for life – especially the eyebrow/facial hair threading.)

After I beautify myself and re-attempt my eye shadows, I'm going to head back to the sweaty villa to figure out exactly who is living in that crusty sleeping bag and using my fridge for their leftovers. And if I find out it's my ex-fiancé, I'm going to be really pissed off.

Date: Thursday
Time: 10:30 a.m.
Location: Leah's terrace.
Day Rating (So Far): Annoying, irritating, and highly emotionally complex.

So much for avoiding Leah for the rest of my un-honeymoon. As soon as I finished making breakfast, she and Jimmy swooped in and took over everything. They were talking all loudly and kissing and being generally annoying and unhelpful.

When I exited the bedroom to try and make my escape, I startled Jimmy so bad that he dropped his glass of orange juice and it shattered and sprayed orange juice all over the kitchen.

"Oops. Sorry," I said.

Jimmy narrowed his eyes at me, then gave Leah a stink eye.

"What are *you* doing here?" he asked me, like a total dick. What did I ever do to him? Besides drink all of his delicious alcoholic beach concoctions and over-gaze into his wonderfully green eyes...

"She's staying here," Leah said, rolling her eyes at his juice-dropping clumsiness. "Someone attacked her two nights ago, left her for dead. Luckily some old fisherman came around and rescued her. Can you believe that? She's lucky to be alive."

Jimmy watched me through his squinty eyes as Leah and I cleaned up the juice and broken glass. You'd think he would have offered to help clean up all the glass and juice he just spilled, but he didn't. He just sat there and watched me through his dumb squinty eyes instead. Ass. Leah's the one who invited me over in the first place! It's not like it's my fault she never told him about it. And, by the way, he's the one dating a ring stealing, sneaky picture taking, fiancé seducing super bitch who is either in cahoots with him, Colin, or both!

I have to get out of this place. All the kissing and loud talking and interrupting of my breakfast is becoming way too annoying to bear. And I'm trying not to take any Xanax today.

Date: Thursday
Time: 5:00 p.m.
Location: Leah's mansion.
Day Rating (So Far): Dangerously close to one of the following: stroke, death, brain explosion, grand seizure, nervous breakdown, secondary stroke, death.

I have absolutely no idea where the hell to even start. My mind is going crazy. The whole entire world is spinning upside down. I don't know who to believe, who to trust, where to go, or how things got so incredibly, stupidly complicated.

I suppose I should start by telling you about my investigatory trip to the sweaty villa, which is where everything went from decently weird to completely messed up.

Of course, everything started off fine, like it usually does.

Recap:
In order to get away from the mansion, I lied to Leah and Jimmy, telling them I had a date with a sexy beach god and that he was going to give me a tour of the island before lunch. I figured, since this had already sort of happened, it wasn't a 100 percent lie and was only a partial lie.

Leah feigned fake-friend interest and asked way too many details about the sexy fictitious beach dweller – How did we meet? What was his name? How were his looks? – and so on. I had to make up so many lies I couldn't even keep them all straight. I'm pretty sure I referred to the made-up date as Lyle, Kyle, and Leo and described him as being both tall and very tall with both brown and red hair. I also said that he was, somehow, from both Kentucky and Brazil. In my defense, lying is very hard, and I really don't know how everyone on this island can keep all their lies straight, especially Leah.

After I got away, leaving a trail of a thousand lies in my wake, I drove back to the sweaty villa. Because I was getting infinity better at being super sleuth-like at all times, I drove past the villa and parked around the corner. That way, to the amateur eye, it would look like no one was home and would therefore give me the situational upper hand. After parking, I walked down the road to the villa and, after triple checking for visitors and attackers, I quickly unlocked the door and leapt inside. I had the weird scary feeling again. The one that said *"You're being watched. You're about to be attacked and hanged off the balcony like René. You're a horrible person who lies and can't keep all of her lies straight."*

I searched the villa up and down, inside and out. I opened up all the cupboards and closets and looked for some clues, instead finding only crusty spices, old towels, and some dead bug carcasses. I inspected the fridge, which had been emptied and cleaned. That was weird, I thought, considering the villa caretaker was supposed to be dead. Who was caretaking in her place?

What if she wasn't really dead and I'd imagined the whole thing?

Frustrated, I revisited the weird under-villa area, poking around at the takeout wrappers and crusty sleeping bag. I found nothing there...other than the old takeout wrappers and the crusty sleeping bag. And the freaking hot water heater! Remember the villa's unfortunate no-hot-water situation? Yeah...that's probably because the freaking hot water heater wasn't plugged in. Grr. I wish I'd known that earlier. I plugged it back in for good measure. Just so the next unfortunate soul who stayed at the villa would be able to take a normal temperatured shower.

As I was messing with the hot water heater, I considered my options. If I were a sneaky ring thief, where would I hide? Maybe there wasn't anyone in the villa at all. Maybe Leah was never harboring Colin in the first place. Maybe the sleeping bag was from some weird homeless construction worker from next door. Aaagh!

I decided to go somewhere less sweaty to review my clue remembering notebook and think about my clues. As I was walking back up the stairs into the villa to get my purse, I noticed something odd. The weird outside closet that held the rusty washer and dryer and all the weird moldy swim gear was now closed. I could swear it had been open before. I *knew* it had been open before.

My heart started to pound.

I reached for the closet door, squeezed my eyes shut, and threw the door open in one elegant swoop.

Then this happened:

1. I opened the door.
2. René's body fell out.
3. It landed right on me.

"Blaaa −" I clamped a hand over my mouth, cutting off my scream. I scrambled out from under the body, pushing it off of me, flailing wildly. The body hit the deck with a dull thud. René's dead bloated face stared up at me accusingly, like it was my fault someone stuck her in the outside villa closet instead of bringing her to a funeral home and informing her family of her end-of-life status. Or whatever happens to a normal dead body.

"Blaaagh!" I bleated into my hand, smothering my scream-like noises. I didn't want any of the next door construction workers to come by wondering what was wrong and finding me wrestling with a dead body. I tried not to smell the sickly stench coming up from the ground, but I did. It smelled like rotting meat and chicken poop.

I scrambled away from the body as quickly as I could, stumbling over my own feet, throwing the back door open, rushing inside, and nearly face-planting into the kitchen counter. I grabbed my purse and rushed toward the front door, fully prepared to just leave René's stiff smelly body lying there where I'd found her. I was about to leap outside and flail my body toward my Jeep when I heard a voice on the other side of the door. And a key turning in the lock. I scrambled backwards, through the kitchen, and into the far back bedroom. I huddled behind the bed in the dark and waited. I could swear I smelled the dead body stink on me. I tried not to barf.

The door opened.

"She was *supposed* to be dead!" a woman's voice hissed. Then, a pause.

"Then why was she at the villa this morning? Not even an hour ago! You told me she was dead!"

Another pause. I peeked my head out from behind the bed. Was she talking about *me?*

A sigh. "I don't know, but we need to move fast. This whole thing is going to shit."

I heard footsteps coming toward the bedroom. Crap. I shifted back behind the bed, finding a tiny crevice only a person my size could fit into.

"What the –" the footsteps stopped. "Someone's been here."

Crap. I'd left the back door open. And the body lying on the deck for anyone to see. Stupid! Any normal 007 would have known not to do any of those things.

"Yeah, I'm staring at her right now," the voice said. "She's on the ground. Someone must have opened the closet door. Dammit! I told you we should have moved the body!"

Pause.

"Why am *I* the one who has to do everything? Get your ass over here and help me move it."

Pause.

"Yes *now!*"

Pause.

"I'll figure something out. It has to look like she did it."

Pause.

"I said I'd figure out something. Just get over here!"

The woman sighed. I heard her step over the body and go into the bathroom. "Anyone here?" she called. The shower curtain rattled. A closet door opened. More footsteps. The bedroom light flicked on. The woman walked into the bedroom.

It was Leah.

Crap.

I cowered behind the bed, trembling. I wished I were invisible. I wished my head looked less like a full moon and more like a decorative pillow. I wished I were a statue, frozen in place and time, without a care in the world. Without a two-timing, panty-stealing, body-snatching, murder-framing, sneaky picture taking scary un-friend.

Leah gave the bedroom a cursory glance, opening the closet doors and peering inside. As she glanced toward the bed, I squeezed my eyes shut, opening them only after I heard her leave the room. The light flicked off.

I let out the breath I was holding. Once I heard Leah head into the kitchen, I tiptoed to the bedroom window, slid it open an inch at a time, and crawled out. Instead of racing to my Jeep, peeling away, leaping onto the next available ferry, and hightailing it home (which is exactly what I wanted to do), I crouched behind a bush and waited.

She was going to frame someone for René's murder. And I'm pretty sure that someone was me. Fucking dick! What did I ever do to her anyway? Why did she have to ruin my life over and over every day? I had to figure out who was on the other end of that phone. I wanted to see who Leah's evil partner in crime was. Was it Colin? Jimmy? Who? And why did they kill poor René in the first place? What did she have to do with any of this?

After a few minutes, a Jeep pulled around the bend, tires crunching. I sunk an inch lower in my hiding spot, peering through the branches. I felt like GI Joe. I wished I had some camouflage face paint with which to paint my face. Then I could disappear into the bush, camouflage-style.

As soon as the Jeep pulled up to the villa, I knew I'd been wrong about everything. My heart sank. The stupid Jeep was green. Emerald green. I closed my eyes and shook my head. Crap. There was only one person I knew who drove an emerald green Jeep. And I'd just fucking slept with him. Dammit!

The Jeep door opened. Eddie hopped out. He looked both ways, his phone pressed to his ear. He was frowning.

"Well I had to do something," he was saying. "She had my wallet. No ID, no credit cards…she was on to me."

A pause.

"I understand."

He hung up the phone and sighed. Then he walked toward the edge of the villa and disappeared down the hill, toward all the under-villa weirdness. I'd bet that's where he and Leah were going to stash René's body. He was probably going to get it all ready and set it up so it would look like I did all of it.

I sat behind the bush, covered my face with my hands, and cried.

When I was finished crying and feeling bad about myself and my super ability to choose the worst possible bed-mates, I scurried back to my Jeep and started driving. Fast. I couldn't sit and watch Leah and Eddie move poor René's body and blame it on me. I couldn't step in and try to stop them either. They'd probably kill me too. I couldn't even go to the police station. The cops already thought I was a big fat liar.

I was stuck. Nowhere to go, nothing to do, and no one to turn to. Soon to be a wanted murderess. Staying with the person who was trying to frame me. Sleeping with the man who was helping her.

Life has once again become a large pile of shit. And I, Sam Stone – no *Sammy* Stone – was stuck right in the middle of it.

Fucking great.

While I was busy feeling sorry for myself, I drove aimlessly from one end of the island to the other. Literally. It took me an hour. I thought about stopping for a monster cocktail at this little spot I saw at the east end of the island, but there were a handful of very scrawny half-feathered chickens pecking around everywhere and a very shady looking gentleman in a straw hat sitting in a lawn chair giving me the stink eye. So, instead, I turned around and drove back toward Cruz Bay. That took another hour.

I eventually found myself sitting in the parking lot at Trunk Bay. Not to relive my oceanic almost-sex with my then-island-sex-god-turned-super-killer-framer, but because it was the last moment of sanity I could remember having before all the attacking and murdering and lies started. Plus, I needed to gather my wits and reflect on the general status of my life and review my sleuthing notebook with the help of a tropical beach setting. Plus, I needed to figure out how to un-frame myself for killing René.

As I settled in at the beach, wiggling hot white sand between my toes, watching the waves lapping the shore, feeling the sand fleas crawl up my butt, I tried to clear my head. Like a meditation sort of thing. I just wanted five freaking minutes to myself, without René and her scary smelly body, without Leah and her stupid evil plan, without Eddie and his sexual powers and un-FBI behavior, without freaking out about my stupid mission and how I was supposed to go home in just a few short days.

But the more I tried not to think about all those things, the more I ended up thinking about them. Then I tried not to think about them even more, but then I thought about them even more. And it ended up being this long vicious cycle I couldn't get out of.

Here's the problem (aside from all my other problems): I don't want to go back home. I hate Elkton and all its stupid small-town lameness. I hate seeing all the dirty sweatshirts and scrunchies all the time. I hate my dumb friends for not being there for me when I needed them most. I hate that, if it weren't for Chomps Douglas, everyone I know would drink themselves to death and overdose on hot dish and adult videos. I don't even like hot dish. I mean, I guess it's okay...

I sighed. Why did Leah and Eddie have to turn out to be such crap-holes? Couldn't anything go my way? Not even once?

After all that work and sleuthing and investment in my great detective notebook, I had nothing. In fact, the only successful thing I've done since stepping foot on this island was successfully believe all the lies everyone told me. Oh, I've also successfully been almost attacked, successfully got hit by a door, and successfully eaten more Xanax than I've ever eaten before in my life.

And in two days I'm supposed to just leave and pretend none of this ever happened. If I can leave after being framed for murder. Come Monday, I'll either be sitting at my little desk in my little cubicle trying to talk people out of sexually harassing each other while simultaneously trying to ignore Kelly and all his super dumbness, or I'll be in some scary lesbian penal colony trying to avoid all the scary lesbians. Just the thought of it makes me want to crawl under something and...well, you know the rest.

Anyway, that's what I was thinking about (mainly) while I was sitting on the beach working on my base tan and getting flea bites all over my legs. Yes, Kelly called *again* while I was sitting there pondering, as if merely thinking about him caught his attention and made him remember that I hadn't returned any of his calls or text messages. And yes, I ignored him. *Again.*

After sitting on the beach for an hour or so, I'd thought of a billion more questions: If Eddie knew that Leah took the ring and I knew that Leah took the ring and Leah and Eddie were cahooting with each other and I was engaged to Colin who was the primo suspect in stealing the ring...why was everyone still sitting in my sweaty villa trying to move dead bodies around? And why did my almost-attacker think I had the ring? Why hadn't he busted in on Leah to take the ring from her – which she most certainly, or at least probably, had hidden somewhere amidst her billion dollar books and sneaky photos? Did the attacker even know about Leah? Was he waiting for Leah to reconnect with Colin so he could get two birds with one stone? And where did Jimmy fit into all of this? Was everyone working together or was Jimmy just a sad sexy bystander? But I'd overheard Jimmy talking about getting the ring! So he *was* in on it, somehow. Right? And why try to frame me for a murder I didn't even do?

I sighed. I sent out a prayer to the Universe/Jesus and asked for help. I wished I'd done my Google researching on how to break Lena Olofsson's stupid evil curse. I sat and stared at the ocean and tried not to cry.

That's when I had the grandest idea of all.

I was going to follow Leah. *I* would catch all the cahooters together. *I* would gather the necessary evidence to clear my name and put Leah and Eddie behind bars. *I* would get to talk to Colin before he was arrested and find out why he lured me into this whole mess in the first place. Not fake Shane/Eddie/Whatever or the super unhelpful island police, *me*.

Bring. It. On.

After that, I got so excited that I ran back to my Jeep and headed straight for Leah's mansion. I wasn't going to go in, for obvious panty-stealing, body-snatching reasons. Instead, I fully prepared myself to commence what I like to call My First Ever Stakeout Situation. Which was a very, very good idea indeed. Or so I thought.

I knew all about stakeout situations from the movies, so the first thing I did was to make sure I was all fueled up and ready to go. Food-wise, that is. This required a stop by the Fishfresh Market, the island's better grocery store, to pick up a few food supplies. Although something about the name Fishfresh seemed very off-putting to me personally. As if a store would sell fish that wasn't fresh? That somehow selling fresh fish was a positive over selling not-fresh fish?

Anyway, I figured that, because it was so hot on the island, I was definitely burning way more calories than I do at home, so I piled on the chips and gummy bears and chewy granola bars and iced coffee drinks and attempted to pay for them with my remaining $12 in cash, trying not to think about how I was going to pay for the cab back to the airport on Saturday. Sure, I still had $12 on my credit card (which had a credit limit of $15,000...yikes), but cab fare would be way more than that. My heart sank. I would be forced to plan for the inevitable dine and ditch type scenario, but with a cab. Not that I've ever done a dine and ditch thing before. (I've totally done that before. Hey, I'm really underpaid and super like eating out.) Unfortunately, my chips and gummy bears and et cetera cost way more than $12 due to St. John's stupidly expensive price tags on food that's really cheap back home, so I put most of it back and ended up with one coffee drink and a lame snack-sized bag of chips. Super dumb.

Once under-fortified with my one iced coffee and smallish bag of chips, I drove back to Leah's mansion and parked firmly out of sight, illegally, half-behind one of the huge bushes lining the road. I was sure that a Jeep parked half into a random bush would not be suspicious in the least.

There seemed to be an inordinate amount of people walking the sidewalks, many more than I ever thought possible. I felt exposed and definitely not at all like I was engaged in a secret covert op. Most of the wanderers ended up walking right past me without so much as a glance, but every sixth person or so would decide to be a total asshole. They'd come up to my Jeep, peer into the windows, and give me weird 'what-are-you-doing-in-there' type looks. This just made me pull my designer sunglasses tighter to my face and wish I'd brought my huge travel novel or a hat or something to make me temporarily invisible. Like that camouflaged face paint from GI Joe.

The thing about stakeout situations they don't show in the movies is how super boring they are. I was bored after exactly seven minutes. Seven minutes after that, I was ready to pull out my own eyeballs. I was just about to whip out my iPad for a blog diary update when the front door to Leah's mansion villa opened. Jimmy stepped out.

Tight jeans, gray t-shirt, muscles like you wouldn't believe, jet black hair, and those startlingly green eyes I could see even from where I sat. God he looked good.

Then I noticed he was wearing gloves. The stretchy white hospital kind.

Then I noticed that his fingers were covered in red paint. Brick red paint.

Or probably blood.

Jimmy looked my direction, and I slid down in my seat, covering my face with my iPad. As I watched from around the edge of the iPad, Jimmy pulled off the bloody gloves and tossed them in Leah's garbage bin. As if he knew nothing about leaving bloody evidence behind. Then he headed toward the street and joined the stream of people walking toward Cruz Bay.

After he was out of sight, I leapt from the Jeep and ran to the mansion, dodging sweaty travelers along the way. I couldn't quite make it there without getting winded, so I had to slow to a walk at the end while breathing heavily and vowing to try exercising more than I currently did, which was never.

Then the door opened again.

I dove behind a bush head first, scratching my arms and face and cheekbones in the process. And probably also messing up my bangs. (FYI – here's the thing about bangs: they look really great for like five minutes, but as soon as you move or go outside, they get all messed up and you start looking like a total asshole who doesn't brush her bangs enough.)

Anyway, I peered out from behind the bush and saw Leah tiptoeing out of the villa. She looked like she'd just stepped off a runway during fashion week. She had on gold sandals, bright white linen pants, and a strappy gold tank that wrapped around her waist and tied at the small of her back. Her hair was up in a sleek bun-thing and her eyes were covered by ginormous sunglasses. I'm not sure how she managed to move a dead body without getting her spendy outfit all dirty. I'd have to ask her later.

Then I saw her gloves. Hospital style, like Jimmy's, but without the blood all over them. She peeled them off and threw them into the garbage. Then she looked around, climbed into a Jeep – not her Jeep, a Jeep I'd never seen before – and peeled off before I could even think to run back to my Jeep and follow her. Damn.

I decided to go inside and do some sleuthing. Why would Leah wear gloves inside her own house? And why would Jimmy wear gloves in his girlfriend's house? And why would they both ditch their gloves outside in the trash can? And why was there blood on only one of the two pairs of gloves? I wondered if other sleuths encountered this many questions on their missions. Probably not. They were probably way better at actually answering some of the questions, instead of just asking all the questions all the time.

I opened the door using the spare key Leah had given me before she turned into a murdering asshole, and tiptoed inside.

"Hello?" I called into the empty kitchen. "Hello? Anyone?"

No answer. My voice bounced off the walls and disappeared into the house, which felt empty and like there were dead bloody bodies just waiting for me around every corner.

I walked into the kitchen, heart galloping, throat constricting, puddle pits reappearing. I fanned my elbows and walked into the living room.

It was trashed.

It was trashed just like Colin's house thing had been trashed. Leather couch cushions torn to shreds, tables overturned, books ripped from the bookcase.

I tried not to think about the blood I saw on Jimmy's gloves, but I did. And it made me go all loose in my downstairs area. Again. Whose blood was that? René's? But wasn't Eddie the one doing the dead body moving? And did people who'd already died even bleed anymore? I wished I'd paid more attention in the movies. And stopped finding more questions to ask.

"Hello?" I called again, heading toward Leah's bedroom and watching for bodies.

No answer.

I thought again about calling the cops, but I hated them. Officer Gregory had totally dissed me and gave me a very bad attitude and called me a liar. How was I supposed to know that the ring I wanted to file a stolen report on was actually an already-stolen $2.2M historical heirloom? My life would have gone a lot better if he had just told me that at the start. Plus, what was I supposed to say if I did actually call them? The girl I'm staying with trashed her own mansion and killed her own crappy caretaker and stole my ring that was already stolen by my ex-fiancé? I'm sure that story would go over great.

Leah's bedroom door was partly open. I reached out to push it open all the way, trying not to notice my super trembly arm and hand movements. The bedroom, too, had been overturned. Sheets ripped off the bed, dresser drawers emptied, and – oh *God* – blood. A pool of blood was congealing on the floor near the closet door. I moved toward it but, before I could take one full step into the room, an arm snaked around my head and a hand clamped itself firmly over my mouth. *Again.*

Before I could curse all that was right with the world, the person behind me flipped me around, and I found myself face to face with Jimmy himself.

Crap.

Jimmy's delicious green eyes bore into mine, but he kept his hand clamped over my mouth so hard I almost suffocated.

"I'm going to take my hand away," he said quietly, calmly. "But only if you swear not to scream."

I nodded, clenching my thighs together until they shook, trying to breathe.

Jimmy took away his hand slowly, and I gulped in a breath of air. My ankle turned. I stumbled. Jimmy grabbed my elbow to steady me.

"Are you alright?" he asked.

I shook my head.

"Are you going to pass out?"

I shook my head again.

"The blood –" I stammered. "Did you touch it? The blood? Why did you touch it? Is it René's? Whose is it?"

Jimmy studied my face. "Here, let's go sit down," he said finally.

I was in shock, I think. I couldn't do anything except let Jimmy lead me back to the living room and sit me down on the torn apart couch. The same couch Eddie and I got dirty on just a few hours ago. I tried not to think about it. I'd slept with a murder accomplice. I'd slept with a dead body mover. I was the worst sort of person in the whole world.

Since all the leather had been torn to shreds, I sat on the edge of the couch frame and teetered there uncertainly. The frame poked into my butt and was generally highly uncomfortable, but I tried to enjoy it, thinking about how much worse a crappy penal colony bed was going to feel.

"What are you doing here?" Jimmy hissed. Then, as I started sobbing all over myself, he asked gently, "Can I get you anything? A glass of water?"

I shook my head. "I– I–," I stammered. My cheeks went pink.

"It's okay," Jimmy said. "Take your time."

I took a deep, steadying breath. "I'm staying here," I said finally. "That's why I'm here. Why are *you* here? Why did you have blood on your gloves? Where did Leah go?"

Jimmy sighed. "Leah and I..." he said. "We..." He sighed again, shaking his head. "After you left this morning, Leah and I grabbed some breakfast. Then I went to check in at the bar. To see if they needed me today. It was slow, so I left after a few hours. When I came back, the door was open. I walked in, saw this –" he waved a hand at the mess – "and then I saw you."

"Did you call her? Where did she go? Whose blood is that? Is there someone lying battered in that closet? Did you check the closet? Who's in there? Where did Leah go? Why did you have gloves on?"

I was on the verge of hysteria. I wished I had eaten my whole bottle of Xanax before looking into that bedroom.

"Shhh," Jimmy said. "It's going to be okay, Sam. Leah's fine. She's fine. There's no one in the closet."

"How do you know?" I demanded. "Did you look? Did you talk to Leah?"

"Sam, trust me. She's fine."

"I saw you leave," I said. "With blood on your gloves. What was the blood doing there? Whose blood is that?"

"I don't know," Jimmy said. "I told you, when I got here, it was like this. I put gloves on so I wouldn't mess up the crime scene." He hesitated, watching me warily. "Why were you watching Leah's villa?"

"I..." I dropped my chin to my chest, shoulders sagging. "I was doing a stakeout," I whispered.

"A stakeout? On Leah?"

"Yeah," I mumbled.

"For how long?"

"Fourteen minutes. Roughly."

"Why?"

"Because she..." Stole my ring! Stole my underpants! Stole pictures of me without permission! Stole my ex-fiancé before he was my ex-fiancé! Is currently framing me for murder! Pick one!

"Because I thought she knew where Colin was and wasn't telling me."

"Colin is the guy who gave you the ring you were wearing when you got here?"

"Yes," I mumbled.

"She doesn't know where he is," Jimmy said.

"How do *you* know that?" I asked.

Jimmy and Leah and Eddie were probably all in cahoots and were trying to kill Colin for taking the fancy ring out from under their noses and giving it to me.

"How much do you know about that ring?" Jimmy asked, ignoring my question.

"Everything," I mumbled.

Jimmy raised his eyebrows. *I don't believe you,* those eyebrows said. *Not even a little.*

"It's true," I protested. Mainly to the eyebrows. "I know about Sapphire Junction. I went there, actually. I spoke with that super old dude. He told me about the DeBlume diamond. The break in. He told me about Colin and Leah. He said that –"

"Whoa, hold on a second," Jimmy interrupted. "Colin and Leah?"

"Yeah," I said. "I saw some naked picture Colin painted of her." I rolled my eyes. "It was called 'Muse' and she was all... naked."

Jimmy frowned at me.

"Did you not know about her and Colin?"

"There is no *her* and Colin. There was never a *her* and Colin." Jimmy's eyes went from sexy and super gorgeous to stone cold killer in the span of one millisecond. Yikes. I decided to test out some distraction techniques to get away from the hard scary eyes and get back to the soft green eyes.

"How does any of this have anything to do with you?" I asked.

"It's complicated," he said, looking at me warily.

"Are you in on the ring stealing too?" I asked. "With Colin and Leah?"

"What are you talking about?" Jimmy looked confused. I decided to try an easier question.

"Are you and Leah actually dating?"

Jimmy nodded.

"Are you really a bartender?"

He hesitated. "I really work there," he said.

"But that's not the only place you work."

He didn't say anything.

"Why were you so concerned about messing up the crime scene?" I asked. "Why did you just happen to have gloves lying around that you could put on? Did you kill René?" My head was spinning. The last question just sort of slipped out accidentally. I knew I wasn't supposed to be asking a potential murderer if he'd murdered someone. Then he would never let me go! Stupid.

"What?" Jimmy was saying. "No, who the hell is René? Are you okay Sam? Do you need to lie down?"

"I'm fine!" I shouted. "*God!*"

I sighed, frustrated. "So where else do you work, besides the Beached Bar?"

"I can't tell you that, Sam. It's classified."

Classified? Crime scene? Convenient gloves? "Next you're going to tell me you're some sort of secret undercover FBI agent too, right?"

Jimmy startled, looking sheepish.

"Seriously?" I shouted, standing up and flailing my limbs about wildly. "You're seriously some sort of secret undercover FBI agent too? Oh my God. I can't believe it! This stupid island. This stupid place! I can't take this anymore!"

"Whoa Sam," Jimmy held out a hand. "Calm down. Sit down."

"Why not just investigate like a normal person?" I shouted. "Whip out your flashy badge and wave it around and get some answers that way. Why all the pretend undercover lies and messing with people's heads and emotions all the time?"

Jimmy shifted uneasily. "It's complicated," he said again. "A lot more complicated than it seems."

"Why me?" I moaned, covering my face with my hands, ignoring my sticky greasy face-skin. "Why does everyone hate me and want me to die?"

Jimmy raised his eyebrows again.

"You're the key," he explained. "You have the diamond."

"*Had* the diamond," I corrected, sitting down again. "I don't *have* the diamond anymore. Leah took it the first night I was here. Stole it right out from under me."

Jimmy's eyes narrowed.

"When I was in the bathroom," I explained. "I overheard..." I stopped, unsure. Confused. "Wait a second..." I said. "I heard you on the phone. I heard you talking to someone about my ring. About taking it from me."

"Yeah," Jimmy said. "Obviously. I want it back. You have it."

"*Had* it," I corrected again. "Leah has it now. That's why her place was ransacked, right?"

Jimmy looked confused. And angry. And sexy. "You don't have the diamond?" he asked.

I put my head in my hands. The world was spinning out of control. Everything was getting so messed up.

"What are you talking about?" I mumbled.

"If you don't have it," Jimmy said. "Who does?"

"*Leah* has it!" I screamed into his face. "Hello? Can you even hear me?"

"Leah doesn't have it," Jimmy said. "If she did...that doesn't even make any sense."

"You think any of this makes any sense to me?" I screamed. "Every time I turn around, something changes. First Colin designed a ring just for me, then it turns out he stole it. I think it's a garnet and therefore treat it all horribly, then I find out it's some super spendy famous diamond ring owned by some rich Italian dude. Colin's place was ransacked, Leah's place was ransacked. A strange man shows up in my backseat and threatens me with guns and dirty rags. You're not a bartender. Shane's name is Eddie. You're both stupid undercover FBI agent lying dicks." I sat down again and burst into tears. "I just can't think straight anymore," I sobbed.

Jimmy stiffened, his body going rigid. "Both FBI agents?" he said. "What FBI agent?"

"You," I sobbed. "And Eddie. Or Shane. Whatever his name is."

Jimmy fell silent. After awhile, I looked up at him through my tears. He was clenching his teeth together, his hands balled up at his sides.

"That's what he said anyway," I said. "Before I saw him with the body. Lying dick."

Jimmy stood up and started pacing. He ran his fingers through his hair over and over until it was all tangled up and greasy.

"What body?" he asked.

"René's."

"Who the hell is René?"

"The crappy caretaker," I whispered. "She looked after my villa. Poorly."

"Eddie was there?" Jimmy asked, looking at me with wide eyes. "With the body?"

I nodded.

"Where is he?" he asked, his voice hard.

"Who?"

"EDDIE!"

The windows rattled. I winced.

"I'm sorry," Jimmy said. "I didn't mean…"

He reached out to touch my shoulder, but I shrunk back.

"Sam," he said. "I'm – I mean Eddie…he's not who you think he is. He's – I need to know where he is. Right now."

"I know that," I said. "I heard him. I saw him. I can't believe I slept with him." My head was spinning even faster. My chips and snacks and iced coffees from earlier threatened to make a second appearance, all over Leah's carpeting.

"Sam, think," Jimmy said. "Where is he? I have to know. He's dangerous. He could ruin everything. Trust me. I know him. Please, tell me where he is." He stared at me with those green eyes and made his lips go all soft and awesome. For a moment, I thought he was going to lean in for a kiss. My belly turned to mush.

"He was at my villa," I whispered. "Last I saw him."

As soon as the words left my lips, Jimmy was up and out the door. He never even looked back to say goodbye, to tell me what I should do next.

So here I am. And that's that.

Comment from MELODY JANE FREEMAN: Um, hey Sam. I'm not sure if I'm doing this right? This is Melody, from back home. Elkton, I mean. Um, I just wanted to tell you that Martha Shaker came across your blog diary and told Faye all about it. Faye told Kathy who told Marge who told

Amanda who told me. There's been a line halfway out the library all day, and I'm pretty sure people are printing your blog diary and making copies for everyone not in the library line. Personally, I think it's pretty cool that you're having so much fun out there and having sex and solving crimes and all that. But there are some other folks here who just aren't too happy about things. Pretty much everyone except me. You should probably call me when you get a second, okay? Don't worry, it's going to be fine. (Hi Mom!! Hi Peder! Look, I'm blogging! I'm doing it!)

Date: Friday
Time: 3:00 a.m.
Location: Scary Ransacked Mansion.
Day Rating (So Far): Oh Holy God.

Why is my life so horrendously unlucky and horrible? I feel like placing large stones in my pockets and wading out into the ocean to die.

Somehow everyone in Elkton has discovered my blog diary. I should have known it was only a matter of time. Especially since I had seven whole followers and a few thumbs up on Reddit, even though I don't even really know what that is. Damn you Martha Shaker! Why did you have to go and open your big fat mouth to Faye Freaking Erickson? Did you not know that it would take her loose lips exactly five seconds to turn around and tell the whole rest of the world?

(Sorry Martha. I actually really like you. But why? Why did you do it? Oh *God*.)

I'm going to be sick all over the place. I can't even think. I don't know what to do. I talked bad about everyone. I talked bad about my parents. My grandparents now know that I think they're mean and old and horrible. Amanda knows I secretly think she's a huge horrendous bitch. Because she is one, really. And all my un-friends know how I really feel about them. And Vera. Poor old Vera. You really aren't that bad at cutting hair, Vera. I mean, you are, but you really can't help it. You're just so old. You should really retire. But then who would cut everyone's hair?

And Kelly.

Oh *God*.

Ignoring his calls was bad enough. But to not call him back and then think all those horrible awful thoughts about him on top of it? Now he's going to read all about it. Everyone in Elkton is going to read all about it. If they haven't already.

I'm going to lose my job. I've likely already lost my job. I've said so many bad things. So many things.

My head is spinning. Life has spiraled too far out of control. It's happening at last. Everything I've dreaded my whole life is now happening before my very eyes. Everyone in Elkton knows about everything. Colin, my stupid un-honeymoon, the fake non-engagement ring, my substance abuse issues, my self-esteem issues – especially in the looks department – and my horrible inability to do anything right. I'm a broke, friendless loser just minutes away from getting framed for a murder I didn't even do.

Now everyone hates me, probably even my parents. I made fun of their old ratty sweatshirts and their lack of technological innovation and their inability to drive me to the airport properly. I made fun of everyone who ever cared about me, just because I thought life would be better on the outside and they were too stupid to notice.

But it's not. Life isn't better on the outside. It's worse on the outside, actually. Sure there's sun and nice weather and beaches and gorgeous men with dazzling smiles and very sexy green eyes...but there are also lies and fake rings and evil thieves and pretend FBI agents who sleep with you and give you the best sex of your whole life and then make you feel bad about yourself for believing all their lies and non-FBI statuses.

Oh God. All I want to do is crawl up under the sheets of my king-sized bed and never come out for the rest of time.

And the worst thing is that my mind is so frantically wild that I have to keep writing this blog diary or my brain is going to implode. I'll have a stroke for sure and then who's going to take care of me?

Forgive me Elkton. Forgive me Mom and Dad. Forgive me mean grandparents (you really are very mean, you know). Forgive me un-friends. Forgive me Kell– ah, fuck it. I still hate you, Kelly. I'm fired anyway. You should know how horrible you are.

I have to type on. There is so much more to this story. My seven Reddit followers and my Ukrainian bride need to know what happens next.

Comment from Lena Olofsson: Hello? Yeah, I have no freaking idea what your talking about. I never put a curse on you. And that boyfriend was Baptist. Not Wiccan. WTF??

Comment from Sam: Really? You never put a curse on me? For real?

Comment from Lena Olofsson: Um…no. I think I would remember doing that.

Comment from Sam: Then who put the curse on me?? Did your boy-friend do it?

Comment from Lena Olofsson: Maybe you put it on yourself.

Comment from Sam: Why would I do that? Aaagh!

Comment from Lena Olofsson: ??

Date: Friday
Time: 4:11 a.m.

I can't believe Lena didn't put that curse on me. I can't believe her boyfriend wasn't a Wiccan. Everything I've believed is un-true. All those bad things just happened to me because…because of something else. Something not curse-related. What the hell? How can I break a curse I don't even have on me in the first place? Am I just that unlucky? God I hope not…

After Jimmy left to go track down Eddie, I was so emotionally destroyed that I could do nothing but drag myself back to the guestroom, pull some sheets onto the ripped-apart bed, crawl up in them, and cry.

I cried for hours and hours and couldn't sleep one single wink. My eyes are now pink and puffy and my forehead is a mess of puffy lines and plastered on bangs.

I can only assume that Jimmy ran out of the mansion to go to the sweaty villa and find Eddie and probably kill him for being a pretend FBI agent and ruining Jimmy's investigations. So I'm now 100 percent responsible for Eddie's death. In addition to everything else I messed up.

It makes no sense. Why would Eddie lie about being an FBI agent? What good did that do him? I already would have gone to bed with him (sorry Mom/Dad). He didn't have to go and make up some dumb fake story and some fake name. Was he back to being a writer, then? Or maybe he was the real thief? But where did that leave Colin? And if Leah and Eddie were in cahoots, why was Eddie looking for the diamond? And are Leah and Jimmy in cahoots or not? Was Jimmy really an FBI man or was he lying too? Was Leah at the heart of everything? Did she double-cross Jimmy like she double-crossed me? Did Colin double-cross her at the start? Who was the original thief? And whose blood was that sitting by the closet that, oh *God*, is just a few short yards away from me?

Don't think about the blood, I told myself. Do not think about it. Close your eyes and breathe deep. There is no blood. You imagined it, just like you imagined René's nasty dead body. You've been dreaming this entire time. You're going to wake up in your bed and it's going to be your wedding day all over again but this time Colin will be there and then you'll spend the whole day laughing about the wild nightmare you had. Okay. Now, wake up!

Crap.

Thinking about the blood, I dragged the dresser in front of the bedroom door and stacked the lamp and vase and a water glass on top of it. It didn't help at all.

My life has gone from reasonably okay to worse than it's ever been before in the whole history of everything. Even my new look and awesome eyebrows can't lift my spirits now.

Maybe a dip in the Jacuzzi tub will help.

Update:
A dip in the Jacuzzi tub did not help.

Every noise has me jumping out of bed and looking for attackers and blood-drawers and scary mansion ransackers. I have to get out of here. I don't know where I'll go or what I'll do, but I have to get out. I'm packing up my stuff and blowing this place, once and for all. I don't care if I have to shack up at the ferry dock until it's time to leave to catch my flight back to – oh God – Elkton.

What am I going to do?

Comment from Amanda: Just so you are aware, I did NOT send you that picture of the billboard so I could prove that my ring is better than yours. I did it so you could see the new billboard picture. I thought you would be excited that they finally changed it. By the way, I knew the whole time that Colin didn't really design your ring. All you had to do was look at it to know that.

Comment from MELODY JANE FREEMAN: Sammy. Oh my God. Are you alright? Everyone here is freaking out. Your mom is telling everyone you've been kidnapped and sold to sex slaves like some girl from Arizona? Is that true? If so, do the kidnappers still let you have your ipod thing? Oh my God. Martha Shaker kept the library open all night so we could all get on the line and do the chats with you. Even though there's a blizzard and Chomps Douglas said for everyone to stay at home. I don't care. I just want you to come back safe. My mom says hi!

Comment from DAD: Sammy? Sammy? are you getting it? hello?

Date: Friday
Time: 4:17 a.m.
Location: Scary Ransacked Mansion, Still.
Day Rating (So Far): TBD

I gathered up enough wits to do some actual 007 sleuthing with help from some deep breathing exercises and several half-Xanaxes. I refuse to let this scary un-honeymoon get the best of me. I refuse to be a victim of horrible circumstance while completely sober. Instead, I will hold my head high, remove the dresser from the door, and investigate the ransackage like a proper investigatory individual.

Date: Friday
Time: 4:21 a.m.

I'm just going to make myself a mimosa first. Just a little one.

Date: Friday
Time: 4:47 a.m.
Location: Scary Ransacked Mansion, still.
Day Rating (So Far): There is someone in the closet.

Oh *God.* The massive mimosa and loads of Xanax provided just enough artificial courage to warrant a trip to Leah's bedroom to double check the blood spatter. I decided to embody *Dexter* and *Breaking Bad* put together and pretend that the sight of blood would not cause any of the following things to happen, even though it did:

1. Major whack attack complete with heart palps and an over-abundance of stress sweating.
2. Tunnel vision and subsequent drop-to-knees/hold head in hands maneuver.
3. Untrustworthy bladder area resulting in wobbly knees and very trembly inner thighs.

After the aforementioned incidences passed, I sat on my hands and knees just inside Leah's bedroom door, listening to the moaning and groaning of the person who lay inside the closet.

Right.

The person inside the closet was probably the owner of the blood. He was also probably the victim of either the ransackers or Jimmy-the-bartender-turned-FBI-agent or both.

Options:
1. Call police (do not know phone number + hate police).

2. Call anyone else staying on the island (do not have anyone's phone number).

3. Run away and hide.

4. Open the closet door.

Right after I decided to pursue option #3, the closet-dweller picked up his moaning and groaning and started calling out for help. It sounded so pitiful, like a dying dog or something. And I just couldn't bear the thought of living the whole rest of my life after turning my back on something that was dying so horrifically and loudly.

So I opened the door. But before I did, I backtracked to the kitchen and grabbed a very large and long butcher knife from Leah's knife rack. And then I opened the door. And then I saw Colin.

"Colin!" I screamed, dropping the knife and rushing into the closet, which was a walk-in and very gargantuan and huge and filled with multi-thousands of dollars of clothes and shoes and purses. Colin was lying on the ground, hands and feet tied together with rope. He lifted his head an inch off the ground.

"Sammy?" he said. Then his eyes rolled back in his head, and he died.

Sorry, let me clarify. He was still breathing and things, so he wasn't actually dead. He was just dead to the world. And by that I mean he went unconscious.

I wasn't quite sure what I was supposed to do, so I Googled "what to do when you find your ex-fiancé unconscious in the closet." After some intelligent researching, I saw one clever trick that said "if the face is red, lift the head and if the face is pale, lift the tail." I checked Colin's face. It was highly pale. I grabbed his legs and propped them up on a shoe box. Then I went back to the Googling.

After splashing water on his face and digging around for some ammonia and waving that under his nose and smacking his cheek every few seconds while yelling "Wake up! Wake up!" into his face, Colin finally started coming to. And I congratulated myself for successfully resuscitating a dead person.

"There, there," I said as he started to open his eyes. I tried to sound very caring and nice when, in reality, I was so mad at him I could have left him in that closet for all eternity. Even so, I got him a towel filled with ice for his head and undid his ropes and helped him sit up. He was very slow and smelled super gross.

"Redo the ropes," he whispered into my mouth. I tried not to barf at the smell of his breath. It was nasty. Like morning breath and old dirty ass, put together.

"Wait, what?" I said. "But I'm rescuing you!"

"He's coming back," Colin said into my ear. (I turned my face away from his mouth just in the nick of time.)

"Who is coming back? Who?"

Colin's eyes fluttered. "Pocket," he said.

"No!" I shouted, shaking him and smacking his cheek and waving the ammonia around and accidentally spilling some on his shirt. "Stay awake!" I cried. "I don't know what to do! I don't know anyone named Pocket!"

"Ropes..." he mumbled. "Can't...save Leah..."

"Save Leah?" I got confused. "She's fine, I just saw her leave."

"Not...Leah...pocket."

Then he was dead again. To the world. Not officially dead. Right.

After that, I wasn't quite sure what to do. But I figured that the last thing I wanted was for the ransacker to come back and find me and Colin there in the closet. If that happened, I would probably end up in the closet, too. Then who would save us?

I ended up retying the ropes, leaving a scissors and butcher knife tucked into a purse, hopefully so Colin could see it but not the ransacker. I went back out to my Jeep, which was still parked half in the bush, and waited. Then I realized what Colin meant when he said 'pocket.' I raced back inside, checked all his pockets, and returned to the Jeep with the contents of his pockets grasped firmly in my fists. Then I waited again.

Date: Friday
Time: 9 a.m.
Location: Joe's Diner.

Day Rating (So Far): So, so horrible. Joe himself even took pity on me and felt so bad that he gave me some free cheesy potatoes to ease my emotional pain.

Guess where I am? Yep. Back at my old stomping grounds. Officially known as the only place on the whole island I feel safe. Only because I can stick myself in the corner with my back to the wall and look at everyone and not be worried about someone attacking me from behind or trying to mug me and ransack my body cavities for the missing diamond.

I've been here since the diner opened, which was three whole hours ago. My butt is sleeping, my legs are cramped, and my veins are likely developing blood clots as we speak. But I'm too afraid and frustrated to even move.

After raiding Colin's pockets, I sat in my Jeep for over an hour, waiting for the kidnapper to return. I felt so bad about leaving Colin there in the closet by himself, starving to death and probably suffering from numerous psychological disorders. Just when I was about to go in and rescue him for good, despite his anti-rescuing protests, I saw a short fat person with slumped shoulders and a hat covering his face rushing down the street toward Leah's mansion. It was so dark I could hardly see anything, but I could see enough to see that the person was too short and too fat to be Jimmy. Then the fat shadowed hunchback went into the mansion, stayed in there for awhile, and eventually came out with a very long and large object – an object shaped exactly like a tall artist with a strong side profile – draped over one shoulder.

Oh *God*, I thought. I've killed him. I've killed Colin. My once true love. I should have gone to the shady police station for help after all. But I didn't want to miss the ransacker coming back. And I didn't want to go back to the shady police station and get yelled at again and probably arrested for a murder I didn't even do.

The figure hobbled to a Jeep parked a few yards down the road. I waited until he had dumped Colin's hopefully still alive body into the trunk before swinging my Jeep around to follow him. I followed him for about four minutes. And then I lost him.

So yeah, that happened. There are only like three roads on the whole island and barely anyplace for Jeeps to go, and yet I lost him. In under four minutes. Why am I so awful at every single thing I try to do? I try to be a good fiancé and fail, I try to be a good solo honeymooner and totally fail, I try to be a mission-capable 007 and fail even more.

When will anything go right for me?

Colin's gone again. Leah's gone. Eddie is likely murdered at the hands of Jimmy-the-bartender-turned-FBI-agent. My flight home leaves in like 24 hours, and I'm condemned to go back to Elkton, where everyone except Melody hates me and read all the bad things I had to say about them.

I'm broke, sunburned, bug bitten, unemployed, slightly better looking physically but slightly worse off mentally, and – in short – I wish I had never come to this dumb loser island in the first place.

In addition, I wish Colin had never got me this iPad and its magical wireless keyboard, and I wish I had never started a blog diary. All it's done so far is make my life one miserable pile of total crap.

Date: Friday
Time: 10:15 a.m.

To kill some time, I decided to go through the contents of Colin's pockets and look for hidden pocket clues. This is what I found:

1. A tube of Chapstik, half used (potential DNA evidence; save for later).
2. A receipt for Fishfresh Market dated May 17 (half pound cheese, half pound deli meat, one loaf bread; potential clue, save for later).
3. A receipt for Manny's Crafts dated May 17 (two picture frames, glue, two bags gemstones; potential clue, save for later).
4. A slip of paper on which I found these words: *Anna - Sugar Ruins, Friday, 6. – PP* (definite clue; analyze immediately).

I got so excited about the note because (1) it was very cryptic and definitely like something 007 would encounter, (2) it was not understandable at all to the human eye but, because I am a better sleuth than average, I knew it had something to do with a meeting place and time, and (3) I truly believe the note is actually a note from Colin himself. How do I know this? Let me answer that question with another question. Have you ever encountered that really annoying couple who laughs at their own internal jokes all the time even though no one else gets the jokes because they're specific to the couple laughing at them? Colin and I have a few internal jokes like that, but we make sure to only laugh at them when we're alone. And 'PP' happens to be one of our internal jokes. Since Colin and I are no longer together and never will be ever again, I'll tell everyone how I know that 'PP' means that Colin is trying to give me a mission-related clue:

On the night we met, after I crashed Colin's art gallery thing, the following conversation unfortunately happened:

Colin: "Hey, do I know you?"
Me: "Er – no, I came with my friend Alice, who is friends with your friend's roommate. Or something."
Colin: "Oh, stellar. Thanks for coming."
Me: "Sure. Well, you know…"
Colin: "Are you an art aficionado yourself?"
Me: "A what?"
Colin (pause): "Do you like art?"
(At this point I finished my first glass of champagne and Colin waved over a bartendress and got me another glass of champagne and that's when I noticed his nice floppy hair and strong side profile for the first time.)
Me: "I *love* art." (I know nothing about art.)
Colin (grinning and very excited): "Oh yeah? What sort of art do you like?"
Me (deer in headlights-like): "Oh… you know… I sort of like it all. Yours especially."
Me (to self): Must drink faster. Much faster.

Colin: "Aw, come on. Something must stick out. Who's your favorite artist?"

Me (touching Colin's bicep flirtatiously): "You, of course."

Colin (smiling and letting me touch his bicep flirtatiously): "Besides me."

Me (slightly drunker deer in headlights): *Craaap. Think. Think. Think!*

Me: "I really like... um... what's his name. You know, the one with all the...colors."

Colin: ???

Me: "Pedro Picasso! Pedro Picasso. For sure. He's my fave. For sure."

(At this point I felt very educated and worldly and downed the rest of my champagne. Then I proceeded to do this):

Me (slurring slightly): "You know, I never did understand what would possess someone to slice off his own ear like that. I mean, would you ever do that? *I* would never do that. Slicing off your own ear... and when you're such a famous artist like Pedro was. Such a travesty."

(At this point I congratulated myself for appropriately using the word 'travesty.' Even though I learned it from watching the movie *Clueless* with Alicia Silverstone and Donald Faison and that dude from *The Princess Bride* over and over like a billion times.)

Colin: "Um...do you want another glass of champagne?"

Obviously there is no such famous artist called Pedro Picasso. Even if I had meant *Pablo* Picasso, which I most certainly did, he is not the same person as Vincent van Gough who was, as I later learned, the artist who reportedly sliced off his own ear.

After I was done being super embarrassed and Colin was done laughing at me and getting me my third glass of champagne and we decided we were meant for each other, the 'Pedro Picasso' joke lived on in our relationship and in our hearts forever. Until Colin dumped me and left me for dead, that is.

Eventually Colin started leaving me little notes, which he would sign 'PP,' instead of 'Colin.' Then I started ending my emails with 'PP,' and so on.

So that's how I know Colin's cryptic note really meant "Save me please from my stupid kidnapping ransacker by deciphering the rest of this note and meeting me at the sugar ruins at 6pm on Friday, which is tonight." Or something like that. Even though he couldn't meet me at the sugar ruins because he was kidnapped.

I chewed on my pen. Maybe Colin overheard his kidnapper set up the meeting, and he was trying to let me know. So I could go and crash the party and figure out all the clues and solve my mission. Yeah, that must be it. But who was *Anna?*

St. John had multiple sugar ruins. I know this from the stupid magazine I read on the way to the island. The one that had my stupid anti-ring ad in it. Which one was I supposed to meet at? And would Colin be there or would all the cahooters be there instead? If all the cahooters were there, what was I supposed to do about it? I was so confused.

A quick Google search gave me the answer to one of my questions. Of the multiple sugar ruins on the island, one was named – conveniently – the Annaberg Sugar Plantation. *Anna.*

I'd solved Colin's highly encrypted code message! Hurrah! Colin obviously knew that I would whip out my ridiculously successful 007 skills and find a way to obtain the note from his pocket, even though he had no idea if I would ever uncover him in that closet but figured I probably would due to my ridiculously successful 007 skills. Then he obviously knew I would decipher the message with the help of Google and some ridiculously successful 007 skills. All in time to crash the party at the Annaberg Sugar Plantation by 6pm on Friday. Which is today. In like eight hours.

Phew!

My horrors at the thought of Elkton reading my blog diary have been slightly yet temporarily overshadowed by the realization that I am, once again, a natural 007 with penultimate detecting and mystery solving capabilities. I really hoped Colin could figure out a way to escape his kidnapper without me. I wished I could have told him about my successful attacker-escape strategy before he got kidnapped.

Alright, I'm off to devour some free cheesy potatoes and whittle away the hours until 6pm. Only eight more grueling hours to go.

Date: Friday
Time: A few minutes past noonish
Location: Surrogate grandparents' villa.
Day Rating (So Far): A clue! I discovered another clue! And some chicken broth too!

Remember after I was almost-attacked and that super old fisherman slammed me in the face with a bathroom door on accident only to save me from concussion and introduce me to my surrogate grandmother, Lupida? Well I remembered that too, while eating my cheesy potatoes and wondering how in the world I was going to sit in that diner and not go anywhere for eight whole hours.

Once the cheesy potatoes helped me remember the fisherman and Lupida, I left Joe's and drove to their villa as fast as my Jeep Wrangler tires would take me. When I got there, Lupida was out in the garden picking tomatoes. Her husband (my rescuer), whose name was Nico, was inside taking a nap.

Lupida met me at my car door like she already knew I was coming. She was smiling broadly and carrying a load of tomatoes in her skirt.

"I hoped to see you again!" she exclaimed, throwing an arm around me and crushing me into her boob folds, despite the tomatoes. I heard a distinctive popping sound and hoped it was a tomato and not an organ or boob of some sort.

"Please, please, come in," said Lupida. "It is too hot today. I have fresh lemonade."

Mmmm, lemonade.

"You have been doing better, yes?" Lupida said after she dumped her tomatoes into a bowl and poured me a giant glass of lemonade. "No more night running?"

Night running? Oh, right. One of my billion lies.

"Sure," I said, slurping my lemonade loudly. "No night running."

"And the chicken broth?" she said. "Are you doing the chicken broth?"

"Um…" I said. Lupida was looking at me all concerned and grandmotherly-like, and I just couldn't bring myself to lie to her about the chicken broth in addition to all my other lies.

I set my glass down. "I wasn't really night running," I confessed. "I mean, I was but…" I burst into tears.

Lupida instantly wrapped me up in her boob folds again, and there was just something about having my face smooshed into some grandma boobs that made me cry even more. By the time I was done, I'd cried so much that the front of Lupida's shirt was damp with tears and my face was a mess of red puffy lines.

My sobs had also woken up Nico, and he shuffled into the kitchen looking concerned and very old and still practically toothless.

"Tell me what happened," said Lupida. She waved at Nico to sit down and poured out two more glasses of lemonade.

And so I did. I told them everything. By the end of my story, our glasses were bone dry and both Nico and Lupida were staring at me like I had two heads and fifteen arms. Then Lupida got up and started heating up some chicken broth.

"Why not just go home?" said Lupida after my chicken broth was done. She gave it to me in a mug, piping hot, to sip at and rejuvenate my insides.

"Money," I said. "For one thing. And not wanting to face all of Elkton."

Nico chimed in. "Ah crab nebba forget 'e hole," he said. Even though I had no idea what that meant.

"Better to die?" said Lupida, ignoring her husband. "To get attacked and scared out of your mind? All because of Francisco's diamond?"

Nico huffed. "Dat family got problems plenty, Lupa. Drag dis poor girl into da mess."

My ears perked up. "What family?" I said. "What problems?"

Lupida *tsked.* "No gossip in this house," she said, giving Nico a stink eye.

Nico scowled. "Yoh is anyt'ing to he?" he said.

"No," said Lupida. "Not that it matters. That man has always been very good to us. Says hello whenever we see him. Always a kind word to you."

"Wait," I interjected. "Wait a second. That Francisco dude is here? On the island?"

Nico nodded while Lupida *tsked* some more.

"Francisco Vitale?" I pronounced it "Vital."

"Vitale," Lupida corrected. She pronounced it "Vee-*tall*-lay."

"*Vee*tillay," I said.

"Vee-*tall*-lay," said Lupida.

"Vee....tilly," I said, frustrated. My mouth couldn't do it the way hers could. Whatever. I wouldn't have to know how to say that dude's last name anyway.

I turned my attention back to Nico, who was nodding. "He just up dat 'ill," he told me, pointing out the window.

"Nico!" scolded Lupida. "The girl's been through enough. Please."

"No I haven't!" I said, shooting out of my chair. "I haven't been through enough at all! I can't believe he's here! He's been here the whole time?" I started pacing, my heart racing. "I have to go see him. I have to talk to him. I have to apologize for losing his family's billion dollar heirloom. I just have to."

And, despite their protests, I'm happy to tell you that that's exactly what I did.

Date: Friday
Time: 4:00 p.m.
Location: Francisco Vitale's ginormous hillside castle.
Day Rating (So Far): Infinity!!

Right. Despite all of the emotionally complex horrors of this unhoneymoon, the last few hours have been the most incredible hours of my entire life. Looking back now, I can almost say that the wedding-day dumpage, solo vacationing, ring theft, almost-attacking, and epical trail of lies was almost worth it to see Francisco's amazing castle and get tea served to me by a real life personal servant. Almost.

Okay, not really.

But close.

Recap:
After leaving my surrogate grandparents' villa, belly filled with delicious lemonade and chicken broth, brain filled with deliciously juicy clues, I headed up Highway 10 in search of Vitale's ginormous hill castle.

Even though St. John only has like three roads, and I've been on all of them, I somehow got all turned around. Probably due to the left hand driving and all the trees and dense tropical foliage and things. But, eventually, I did find it. Thank God.

At the entrance to the driveway was a fancy security gate and a little intercom thing. I swung my Jeep around the corner and pulled up as close to the little intercom thing as possible. I wasn't quite sure exactly what to do, so I waited. And waited. And waited.

"Um, hello?" I finally yelled.

No answer.

"Hello? Anyone?"

Nothing.

I noticed a little button at the bottom of the intercom thing that said 'Call.' So I pushed it.

Nothing.

I pushed it again and held it down while yelling "Hello?" every few seconds. Then I let go of the button and kept saying "Hello? Hello?" Just to make sure all my bases were covered.

Finally the intercom thing started buzzing and crackling.

"Hello?" A voice called out of nowhere.

I startled, looking around. "Um…?"

"Who's there? Who is that?"

"Who are you?" I asked finally. "Where are you?"

"I'm here," the tinny voice said. "And you are there."

A long pause. "So…" I finally said. "Hello?"

"Are you the American?" the tinny voice cracked through again.

"Huh?" I asked. "American? Yeah. Yes. I'm American. I'M AMERICAN!"

After a long pause, I heard a loud buzzing sound. Then the gates started opening right in front of my eyes! Once they were fully open, I pulled the Jeep through and drove up the massively long driveway. Then I saw the castle. Then I nearly deuced in my pants. The place was bigger than all of Elkton put together! All stone walls and turrets and huge windows and wings and doors everywhere. I had walked right into an episode of *Downton Abbey.* I wondered if I'd have the opportunity to pull one of those little curtains like the *Downton Abbey* people got to do and if pulling the curtains would cause a personal slave to appear in front of my eyes like magic, like what happens in *Downton Abbey.* I was so excited about the curtain pulling, I forgot to be nervous. For the first time ever, I didn't even have the littlest craving for Xanax.

I pulled up to what I figured was the front door. There was a little man standing there wearing all black with a little black hat on top of his head. As I pulled up next to him, I furiously wished with all my might that:

- I lived in a ginormous hill castle in the middle of a tropical island complete with little men in hats standing near doors to greet my visitors for me.
- I had showered and redone my bangs and hair and applied my eye shadow.
- I had infinite sums of dollars and was generally way more elegant and awesome than I actually am.
- I had put on way better clothes. Way, way better clothes. (Pretty much anything better than the ratty jean shorts and old gray tank top with the phrase 'Hang Tough' on it that I was wearing.)

When I pulled to a stop, the little man hopped over and opened the door for me. Then he put his hand out and I became very concerned that he wanted some dollars from me that I didn't have. But then he said in a very British voice:

"The keys, Madame."

Right.

I gave the little man my keys and he hopped in, driving my car away like a real live chauffeur or valet or something. I walked up to the front door. Before I could even knock, it swung open and a little man wearing all black with a little black hat on was standing there with a smile. I got so confused. How could the little man have parked my Jeep and ran around inside the house to open the door for me in like half a second? Was he a magical little man?

The man's smile wavered a bit when he saw me, probably because he was blown away at how awesome my 'Hang Tough' tank top was. Then he recovered and did a little bow and waved me inside.

"This way, Madame," he said. I tried not to grin. No one had ever called me *Madame* before. I felt so grown up and exotic! I shook my bangs a little bit for good measure.

The little butler man led me down a long skinny hallway with massive oil paintings on the walls and little tables filled with old dusty vases and clocks and things. I was starting to feel less grown up and exotic and highly out of place instead. I was thinking about turning around, going back to my Jeep, and rummaging through my luggage for a dress or my designer sunglasses or something.

The butler man asked me my name, then brought me to a massively huge room with wicked high ceilings and way more paintings than the hallway.

"Samantha Stone," he announced as we walked into the room. Then he did another little bow and walked away.

"Samantha, my darling."

I looked up to see an elderly gentleman dressed in pressed khakis and a starched, dark blue collared shirt walking toward me. He was tall and tan, with a thick shock of white hair and ruddy cheeks.

"I've heard so much about you." The strange man grabbed my elbows and kissed me on both cheeks. Then he held me at arm's length and looked me up and down.

"Well aren't you just a pint-sized thing," he said with a grin and a very heavy Italian accent. He smelled like whiskey and spendy cigars and endless amounts of money. I liked him immediately.

I wasn't quite sure what to do while he had me in hand, so I just stood there grimacing. And wondering how he'd heard all these mysterious things about me when I'd practically never heard of him before.

"Hang tough," he said, looking at my tank top. Then he tipped his head back and roared. "You young people these days."

He sat down on the couch and crossed his legs. "Bates!" he yelled. "Some tea for the young lady! Some whiskey for me!"

Then he turned to me. "So," he said with a frown. "What brings you to my doorstep, my dear?"

"Um," I stammered, feeling my cheeks flush. "I – who – who are you, exactly?"

The old man tipped his head back and roared again. "Who am I, she says." He looked at me with a grin. "You young people these days. I'm Francisco, you see. Francisco Vitale. I heard you had my ring. *Had* being the operative."

Right. "Yes," I stammered. "Had. Right. You see, that's why I'm here. I just wanted to apologize, you see."

"For?"

"Er – um, for…" I had lost all my words. The room was so huge and imposing and the ceilings were so high. I felt like I was in a museum and an incredibly fancy hotel all at the same time. I glanced around at all the huge portraits on the walls and the expensive carpets and curtains and vases and things. I wondered which curtain to pull to get the little man to appear. I could feel Vitale's eyes studying me.

"For?" he prompted again.

"For the diamond," I blurted out. "The DeBlume. I know it was in your family for like a trillion years and that it's worth more than I'll ever make in my lifetime. In fact, it's probably worth more than *me*. I guess that's why everyone keeps trying to kill me over it. But I don't even have it! I *had* it. That's true. Colin – that's my ex-fiancé – he gave it to me. As an engagement ring. Only I didn't know that it was your ring. I didn't know it was *the* ring…"

I trailed off as Bates came in with the tea and whiskey. Oh how I wished that I lived in that huge castle and could order people around and have people wait on me all day. That would be so much better than pretty much anything I could ever think of.

"I didn't mean to lose it," I stammered. "It was stolen. I would have taken better care of it. Had I known what it really was. But I didn't. Not until it was too late."

Vitale held up a hand to stop me. Then he picked up his glass of whiskey and handed it to me. "Drink," he said. "You need it more than I do."

I drank it in two big gulps. Then I coughed, sputtering bits of whiskey all over his huge fancy carpet. He didn't seem to mind.

"My dear," he said, the words rolling around in his mouth like marbles. "There are things in life that, sometimes, just happen. There is no reason for it. No one to blame. The diamond was part of my family, yes, and we treasured it. But now it is gone. And if that is the way it is, that is the way it will be. No use feeling guilty over something you cannot control."

"Really?" I said, my eyes going all dumb and swimmy. "You forgive me? Just like that?"

Vitale stood, motioned for me to stand. "My dear," he said again. "When the ring was stolen, I had hoped the police would recover it and return it to me. But, as the months passed, I realized that relying on the police would get me nowhere. It is, as they say, like idiots leading imbeciles. No one knows ass from elbow."

I stifled a grin.

"So I engaged a – what do you say – a detective. But he gets nowhere. It seems like the ring just disappears. Then I give up hope. And when you arrive, everyone becomes crazy. Thinking you are the one who took it, such a little slip of a girl you are. But my detective, he says no. He says you were tricked. Then we find out that the stone is a fake. And so we are back at the beginning."

While Vitale was blabbering, I had drifted off into the land of my own imagination, gazing at all of the super spendy artifacts all over the place. It took a moment for what he said to register. When it did, I nearly tripped and fell all over myself.

"Did you say that the diamond in the ring was a fake?" I asked. "As in..."

Vitale nodded. "Not real," he clarified. "Fake. A synthetic. Not a diamond. The setting was verified, yes, but the stone had been swapped."

"But..." I faltered. How did he know that?

"When my detective recovered the ring," Vitale started, answering my unspoken question, "we of course had it analyzed straight away. That's when we learned you had nothing but a worthless gemstone. The setting is mine, you see. But the stone had been swapped."

I was speechless. The ring was a fake. After all that, I never had the DeBlume at all. I wasn't actually responsible for losing a cajillion dollar museum piece. Hurrah! But...instead of feeling better about wearing it around the whole time and not taking care of it and banging it into things and sticking it down the garbage disposal, I realized that I had actually started feeling sort of special and important about having temporarily owned such an expensive and historically awesome ring. Realizing that it was a super fake the whole time just made me feel more depressed and lame than I already was.

And the questions. All the questions.

Did Hanson have the fake ring on display at the gallery? Did Colin steal the ring knowing it was a fake? Or did he steal the ring and then switch out the real diamond with a fake stone? Did he even steal it or did he come across it after the stones had been swapped and the setting discarded? When Leah stole the ring from me that night in the bathroom, did she know it was fake? Or did she find out afterwards? Was she the detective Vitale was referring to? What about her day spa?

And the ultimate, million – no, two million – dollar question: Where was the real diamond? Someone had it, and someone else was looking for it. Desperately. They were willing to ransack and bludgeon and kill for it. Why?

I tried to refocus on Vitale, to get my eyes to stop swimming, when, all of the sudden, the room started to shrink in on me. The huge portraits of men in white wigs and funny red pants holding dead birds were staring at me. The regal women in puffy sleeves and starched updos and thin lips were smirking at me and judging me. Everything was starting to go dark and blurry and –

"What the –" My eyes glued themselves to a ginormous painting hanging beside one of the floor to ceiling windows. It was of Vitale and two young women holding bouquets of that flower Leah had been talking about. The kind Jimmy gave her. Bougainvillea, or whatever. But that's not what I was looking at. I was focused on the two identical looking women with brown, glossy hair and wide, dark eyes instead.

"Oh *God*," I said.

"Ah," said Vitale, standing behind me. He clasped a hand on my shoulder. "Aren't they lovely? My granddaughters. Twins. You can barely tell them apart. Anna, on the left. Seven minutes younger than her sister. My Leah."

Leah.

Leah V. de Medici.

V for Vitale.

My mind started racing.

I've heard so much about you.

I saw you yesterday, just off the ferry dock. With Jimmy.
I don't think so. I was working.

There is no her *and Colin.*

Why would Leah ransack her own mansion?

Twins. You can barely tell them apart.

Save Leah.

Before I knew what was happening, my knees buckled and, suddenly, everything went black.

PS – This means that Leah actually *was* trained by spendy European tutors while living in mansions and enjoying afternoon tea. Dope! I mean laaaame. I hate her! She's so amazing.

I hope she's still alive.

When I woke up a few moments later, three little men dressed in black with little black hats hovered over me. Vitale was looking down on me with a white, panicked face.

"Get her to the couch," he ordered. "To the couch."

"I'm fine," I protested, as the men tried to lift me, awkwardly. "I'm totally fine."

And it was true. I was fine. I was better than fine. For the first time all week, everything suddenly made sense.

"Mr. Francisco," I said breathlessly, waving off the men and climbing unsteadily to my knees. "Vitale, I mean." I accidentally pronounced it "Vital" again. I took a breath. "Your excellence, or whatever. I know where the diamond is. I know everything. I know where your diamond is. Or I think I do, anyway." I said. "I mean, I'm like 87 percent sure I know where it is. Please, your...Honor. I need your help."

Part Three
The Time I Put All the Clues Together and Was Generally and Consistently Amazing (For The First Time Ever)

Date: Friday
Time: 6:00 p.m.
Location: Annaberg Sugar Plantation Ruins.
Day Rating (So Far): To be determined based on the outcome of the next few minutes.

So I found out that not only was Leah the granddaughter of the fancy ring-owning Italian dude, she had a freaking twin sister. Named Anna. Apparently, Leah and Anna are *identical* twin sisters who both live on the island but who hate each other furiously. I can't believe I fainted. That was so lame and anti-007 like.

Anyway, I quickly came up with what I thought was a super great mission-successful game plan and explained it to Vitale and his little men. Then Vitale made a phone call.

After his call, I said my goodbyes and made my way to the Annaberg Plantation. To see about the cryptic note that I found in Colin's pocket and to put my really great 007 plan into motion.

So here I am. Signing off. For maybe the last time. Or maybe not. It all depends on how flawlessly my plan works and how awesome I am at solving crimes and missions and things.

Wish me luck.

Date: Friday
Time: 7:45 p.m.
Location: Annaberg Sugar Plantation Ruins.
Day Rating (So Far): Read on, fair soldier. Read on.

When I arrived at the ruins, there was no one in sight. The only thing I saw were sad, crusty brick buildings long fallen into disrepair. I walked up from the road into the ruins, slapping at a mosquito that had landed on my cheek, wishing I'd brought my bug spray instead of leaving it in my Jeep Wrangler along with my iPad and the rest of my travel possessions.

I crunched around the place for awhile, wandering aimlessly and looking for suspicious characters. The sun was setting quickly and, soon, it would be almost too dark to see. I paused, closing my eyes, praying that my plan would work. I slapped at another mosquito.

Behind me, a branch cracked. I spun around. No one there.

To my left, another branch cracked. I spun to the side. Nothing.

I started to get really nervous.

As I was standing in the middle of the ruins, slapping at mosquitoes and praying my plan would work, I heard a voice behind me.

"Sam," the voice hissed. I spun around.

"Shane? I mean...Eddie?" My former tropical island not-dead sex god stepped out from the shadows. I gasped.

What was *he* doing here? I thought Jimmy had gone after him earlier, after I busted his probably-fake FBI cover!

"What are you doing here?" I hissed. "If you came for the diamond, I don't have it. I was lying. Go away!"

"Sam," Eddie held his arms out, palms forward. "What are you talking about?"

"I had Vitale call Anna," I said. "He told her I'd fessed up and knew where the diamond was. I told Vitale to tell her that I found the note and planned to meet Colin here to convince him to turn himself in. Even though he was really kidnapped and left for dead in the closet. I left that part out. For the purposes of the plan. Whatever. Where is she?"

Eddie looked confused. "Anna, Vitale's granddaughter? How would I know where she is? What plan? You found Colin?"

"You didn't come with Anna?" I ignored the rest of his questions.

Eddie shook his head.

"Then tell me how you knew I was going to be here. Or I'll cap your ass."

Eddie's cheeks went red. "I followed you."

"How? No one followed me. I triple checked."

"Well...I sort of put a tracker on your Jeep. And Vitale called me –"

"What?!" My voice bounced off the branches and scared off the mosquito that was busy gnawing at my neck. "You put a tracker on my Jeep? When? What does that even mean?"

"Sam, it doesn't matter. What the hell are you doing here by yourself?"

"She's here to tell us where the diamond is."

Jimmy the bartender-turned-maybe-FBI-agent stepped out from behind a tree. He was holding a gun. And pointing it at the back of Eddie's head. I gasped.

"I should have taken care of you when I had the chance," Jimmy said to Eddie. "Back away from the girl with your hands where I can see them. Sam, are you okay?"

"What?" Eddie said. "What are you talking about?"

"Just do it Shane," I said. "Or Eddie. Whatever your name is."

"Sam, I –" Eddie looked confused. And hurt. And highly sexy. "But..."

"I said back up!" Jimmy took a few steps forward and clicked the safety off the gun.

"Do it!" I cried. "Don't make him shoot you!"

The plan was going awry. Very awry. It was only supposed to be me and Anna and the cahooters. And Colin, if he managed to escape his kidnapper. What the hell was everyone else doing? Besides crashing my stupid plan!

Eddie took a step backward toward Jimmy. He raised his hands. "You can't honestly believe this guy," he said to me. "Do you?"

I looked away, feeling guilty. How the hell was I supposed to know what to believe anymore? The only thing I could ever count on was everyone lying to me all the time.

"But our night," Eddie said, taking another step backward. "Didn't that mean anything to you?"

"It meant something to you?" I hissed. "Is that why you just left without saying anything? Is that why you just disappeared again for the billionth time? Oh, and did you just *forget* to mention that you were planning on heading to my villa? To participate in moving dead bodies around and framing me for it? What the hell?! Who *does* that?!"

(Hint: I'll tell you who…assholes.)

All of the sudden, Eddie was within fighting distance of Jimmy and, in one elegant swoop, he spun around, grabbed a gun from his waistband, and pointed it at Jimmy. A true Western style standoff type situation ensued. This was not the way my great plan was supposed to go. Crap.

"What did you tell her?" Eddie asked Jimmy.

"I told her who you really are," Jimmy smirked. "You're no FBI agent. You're a has-been. You're nothing. No one even knows you're still here. Sam's going to tell me where the diamond is, and you're getting a hole in head."

"Stop!" I shouted. "Shane…Eddie…Jimmy. Everyone just stop! Who's the real FBI agent here? Is anyone? Or is everyone just FBI-faking?"

Eddie looked sheepish. Jimmy looked at me and grinned.

Eddie clicked off his safety and my heart skipped. *Abort plan! Abort!*

"Drop your weapon," Eddie said.

Jimmy laughed. "Drop yours."

They were so busy trying to kill each other, they seemed to have forgotten all about me. I retreated to my initial hiding spot where I'd stashed a very critical piece of my final mission: a .243 Winchester Bolt-Action rifle. On loan from Vitale, borrowed from his very impressive stash of fight-worthy weapons. Just so happens to be the same model I use when deer hunting. That's right. I had you fooled into thinking I had no skills whatsoever, didn't I? Well, like most small town Minnesotans, I hunt deer. And pheasants. And turkeys, sometimes. Mainly deer. And I'm pretty good at it, too.

I picked up the rifle in one elegant swoop and looked back and forth between Eddie and Jimmy. Those idiots were still having their dagger eye death stare down, wondering which one would pull the trigger first.

"You assholes can both drop your weapons," I said. My voice came out hard and awesome, like I really *was* a bona fide 007 about to put a cap in someone's lying ass.

The guys paused their standoff to stare at me. Eddie looked surprised. Jimmy chuckled. "Like you know how to shoot that thing."

"I'm twenty-eight years old," I said. "That makes it…oh, fifteen years of deer hunting. Fifteen years, twelve deer, lots and lots of venison in my freezer."

I looked back and forth between the guys. Who should I be shooting?

My mind started to race.

So, how long have you and Jimmy been together?
About…almost a year, now. He moved here last winter.

It was stolen during the auction. We have one every May.

I heard you talking to someone about my ring. About taking it from me.
Yeah. Obviously. I want it back.
I want it back.

They've found nothing. Nothing at all. Neither has E.J.
E.J. must have sent you.
Detective Stone.

So I engaged a – what do you say – detective.

Vitale called me.

Special Agent Edward Jacobson, of the Federal Bureau of Investigation.
Edward Jacobson.
E.J.

I set my aim and looked straight down the barrel into Jimmy's gorgeous green eyes. "Shooting a dick in the face can't be that different than shooting a deer in the heart, can it?"

Then the plan went even more awry than it already was. Eddie was spending too much time looking at me in awe, and Jimmy took the opportunity to get the drop down on him. He pistol whipped Eddie in the head and knocked the gun out of his hands. Eddie dropped to his knees. Jimmy put the gun to Eddie's forehead.

"Your boyfriend is dead!" Jimmy shouted. "You stupid fool! You're ruining everything!"

"Don't do it!" I screamed. "I won't tell you where the diamond is if you pull that trigger."

"Put your weapons down!" A voice shouted out from behind Jimmy. "Everyone. Weapons down. Now."

A police officer stepped out of the trees. The sun had dipped below the horizon and the light was going gray. It was hard to see anything anymore. But I could see the officer's starch white uniform clear enough. And the gun that he was holding, too. Pointed directly at me.

I put my rifle on the ground. I knew better than to mess around with the police, especially when it came to weapons and things.

"It's him," I pointed to Jimmy. "He's the one you want."

Jimmy, too, had taken the gun away from Eddie's head and had it pointed to the sky.

The police officer stepped toward me. "Are you alright?" he asked.

As he moved toward me, I caught a glimmer of his ring in the moonlight. His pinky ring. He was the guy Officer Gregory was speaking to at the police station! Then, something else. The faded memory of seeing that same glimmer in – oh *God* – the rear view mirror of my rental Jeep Wrangler. It was him. My sausage armed almost-attacker. Officer Gregory's partner. The short fat hunchback who kidnapped Colin and hopefully hadn't killed him yet.

Oh *God.*

"It's a trap!" I screamed. "Eddie!"

But it was too late. Jimmy had his gun re-pointed at Eddie, and I had given up my rifle due to police officer orders. Now Colin's kidnapper had his gun pointed straight at my brain. This meant that all the good guys had guns pointed at them and all the bad guys had all the guns.

This was not the way it was supposed to go.

"Where is it?" the kidnapper asked. "Where's the diamond?"

"Where is Colin?" I countered. "If he's dead, I'm not telling."

"He's not dead," the kidnapper said. "Not yet."

"Show me."

The kidnapper laughed and took a step closer. "Not likely."

"Then there's no deal," I said.

"I'll shoot you if you don't tell me where the goddamn diamond is like now!"

"Do it," I said. "Then you'll never know."

"Dammit!" the kidnapper roared. He turned and glared at Jimmy, who had Eddie on his knees and the gun pointed at his forehead. "This is all your fault."

"How is it *my* fault?" said Jimmy. "It was *your* plan that went to shit!"

"*My* plan?" the kidnapper said. "You're the one who came to me!"

"Shut up!" I screamed. "Shut! Up! *God!* You two are worse than my grandparents. Who cares whose plan it was? Tell me where Colin is or the deal is off. You have two seconds to decide."

(Damn, I was good. 007 couldn't have done it better himself.)

"One, two," said a voice from the shadows. "Boo hoo."

Then Leah stepped out from behind Jimmy with a gun of her own. No, not Leah. *Anna.* Damn. They looked exactly like each other. Identically awesome and super gorgeous with equally great and shiny hair. Dumb.

"There you are," I said. "I was waiting for you to show up."

"Were you now?" said Anna. She looked at me and wrinkled her nose. "Why my sister decided to befriend you, I'll never know. Nice shirt."

"Thank you," I said, glancing down at my 'Hang Tough' tank top. "Nice face."

"What?" she said.

"Never mind."

Turns out, Colin didn't actually write that note that I found in his pocket. Jimmy did. To meet up with his cahooter, Anna, Vitale's *younger* granddaughter. The sister to the rightful heir of the DeBlume diamond, which would be Leah. The chick I saw leaving Leah's mansion after she and Jimmy had ransacked it, looking for the diamond and stashing Colin in the closet. The chick who tried to frame me for René's murder.

Of course, I would have realized earlier that Colin didn't write that note if I had actually taken the time to appropriately investigate it and look at the handwriting instead of just glancing at it and letting Google do the rest. He must have grabbed it and shoved it in his pocket, hoping it would turn into a clue, which it did. He was so smart sometimes!

"So what's your story?" I asked Anna, trying to ignore the guns pointed my way, trying to buy myself some time so I could figure out what to do next. Eddie kept attempting to catch my eye, but I kept ignoring him due to all the guns pointed my way.

"You wanted the ring for yourself, right?" I said. "You knew Leah would inherit it, being older and way more awesome and better looking than you. So you picked up Jimmy and convinced him to cahoot with you, right? Then you – what – had Colin paint dumb pictures for you so you could pass them off as Patrick Patrick's? Which is the stupidest artist name ever, *Jimmy.*

Then you used the auction night as a way to get into the gallery and steal the ring unnoticed. You were the subject of some of the paintings, right, so no one would wonder why you were there. What sort of person steals from her own family? By the way, did you kill René or did you get your fat smelly henchman to do it? What did René ever do to you?"

Anna's eyes were dark and wild. A branch cracked behind me and she swung her gun around wildly. "I had nothing to do with her," she hissed. "That stupid ass thought it was *you*." She glared at the kidnapper. "This whole thing would have worked, too, if your *stupid* fiancé had just played nice. Instead, he swapped out the diamond and left us with nothing." She looked at me and spat at my feet. "Now he's going to lose everything."

She took a step forward in the dark and her ankle turned. As she slipped, the gun wavered in her hand. Jimmy moved to try and grab her before she fell. He failed, and Anna went down hard. *Awww*, stupid two-timing, idiot ring thief failure.

I caught Eddie's eye and he exploded, popping up and doing some fancy non-FBI karate maneuvers on Jimmy to wrestle the gun away. Meanwhile, the kidnapper was distracted and Anna was on the ground, and there was a second where no guns were pointed at me. I leapt sideways behind one of the old crusty buildings and took cover. Just in time. I heard the first gunshot like a millisecond later. About a billion gunshots followed. I curled my body into a fetal position, head in hands, hearing bullets fly around me, just waiting to get shot. Everything was going wrong. *Again.*

Then I heard a voice roaring above all the gun shots. A very familiar voice.

"Don ebben tink aboot id!" A man stepped out from behind the kidnapper, and I popped out from behind my hiding spot to see what was going on.

"Woot!" the voice said. "Woo hoo! All yoo put yurr guns down now!"

"Chomps Douglas?" I shouted. "What are *you* doing here?!"

Chomps glared at me, and I grimaced, looking at the scene. Eddie had Jimmy on his knees. The kidnapper had a gun pointed at Eddie, Chomps had a gun pointed at the kidnapper, and Anna was nowhere to be seen.

"Get da gun," Chomps said, gesturing to the rifle that had fallen near his feet. I grabbed it.

"Shoot da guy," he said.

"Which one? Jimmy or the kidnapper?"

"Might as well ged 'em both."

"Wait!" Jimmy said. "Wait! Don't shoot me. I had nothing to do with this. It was all Anna. It was all her. And *him*," he said, looking at the kidnapper. "*He's* the one who had the buyer lined up. Tell them, you dick."

"Shut up," growled the kidnapper, swinging the gun toward Jimmy's head. Chomps pounced on him and, in one elegant swoop, he had the kidnapper down on his knees and in handcuffs. Then he looked at me and grinned.

"Woot!" he hollered. "Now dat's a story for da boys back home." He slapped a mosquito off his cheek.

"Chomps!" I rushed toward him. "What the hell? What are you doing here? How did you find me?"

"Yurr dad sent me," he said. "Talkin' aboot you been kidnapped and sold for sex or sometin'. I came ta getcha." He gave the kidnapper's sausage arm a turn and the man groaned. "Is dis da guy who gabe you da sex?"

"No!" I said. "Gross. How did you know where I was, Chomps?"

"Er –" Chomps said, standing up and brushing dirt and leaves off his knees. "I mighta read your...diary thingie on da plane on da way here. Martha Shaker printed it off furr me. I ran into yurr fisherman at da ferry dock. Ya know. Nico. Da one who rescued ya? From da sex?"

I nodded.

"Well," Chomps said. "We got ta talkin' and I said I was comin' for ya and he pointed me to...ah...some old Italian guy. So I went to da old guy's castle and he said you were gonna be here to meet up with someone about da ring and stuff. So here I am."

Right. So Nico saved me twice in one week. I really should send him a gift basket or something.

Meanwhile, Eddie had finished doing his tying up of both Jimmy and the kidnapper and came over to introduce himself to Chomps.

"Eddie Jacobson, PI," he said with his hand outstretched. "Nice work."

"Chomps Douglas, Elkton PD," Chomps said, his barrel chest puffed up like a peacock. "Nice work yurrselv."

"So you're not with the FBI?" I asked. "Really?"

"I *was* with the FBI, but I got fired," Eddie said, frowning. "The day we were..." He looked at Chomps. "At the beach," he finished. "Vitale kept me on the case as his private detective though."

So *that's* why he was so rude after our beach make out session! It didn't have anything to do with me after all. He'd just gotten fired from the FBI! Hurrah!

"And Jimmy?" I asked, relieved that Eddie was maybe not as emotionally bipolar as I'd once thought. I mean, I would've been upset too. If I'd just been yelled at by some strange chick and then fired moments later from a really decent job.

Eddie shook his head. "Jimmy was never FBI. I can't believe he said he was."

"Actually...come to think of it," I said, remembering our conversation in Leah's ransacked mansion. "Yeah. That was me. Sorry."

"Are you the one who told him where I was?"

My cheeks went pink. I was really glad for the dark and for my previously awesome standoff handling skills. "Sorry," I said again. "He said you were lying. Which you *were.* How was I supposed to know?"

Eddie sighed and gazed into my eyes. "He almost shot me, you know. You led him right to me."

"Sorry," I breathed. "I thought...you showed up after Leah – I mean Anna – called someone to help her move René's body and frame me for her murder. I thought she'd been talking to you."

Eddie shook his head. "I've been staying at the villa for the last week."

"You're the one who's been staying there? In the sleeping bag?"

Eddie nodded.

"You're the one who put the stuff in the fridge and the dirty dishes in the sink?"

He nodded again. "I cleaned it up though…after a while."

"So you were in the under-villa area while Anna and her sausagey henchman were moving René's body?"

Eddie nodded, cheeks flushing.

"You didn't notice anything?"

"Well, I was sort of…we had just…I was distracted. Then Jimmy showed up to try and kill me."

"Sorry again," I mumbled. "That would have been really horrible, you know. If you'd been shot."

"I know," he breathed. "You too."

We had a long, romantic eye-gazing moment. I nearly leapt on his chest and clawed off all his clothes, to make up for the sex we lost out on when he left me by myself in Leah's mansion.

Chomps cleared his throat.

"Right," I stammered, taking a step back. "So…now what? We've got two guys tied up, one missing ring thief, and one missing ex-fiancé."

"I found Colin," Chomps said. "On da boot."

"Da boot?" Eddie asked.

"The boat," I translated. "What boat, Chomps?"

Chomps proceeded to explain that, while he was making best friends with Nico and having casual conversations at the ferry dock while I was busy trying to solve all the clues and not get shot, Nico mentioned that, while he was out searching for fish, he'd seen the "other American" get loaded onto a boat by "that bartender" and "the fake policeman." Apparently, Nico said, another body was loaded onto that boat, too. A dead one. So Chomps told Nico to go investigate and to not let the boat out of sight. Poor René. At least I wouldn't have to worry about un-framing myself for her murder, since Anna had confessed in front of everyone that she'd had her sausage-armed scary policeman henchman kill René by accident.

Awesome.

In any event, Eddie (or E.J., as Vitale calls him) clapped Chomps on the back, congratulated him for his "excellent police work," and loaded Jimmy and the rogue police officer into his Jeep for whatever happens after bad guys are arrested. Chomps agreed to go recover Colin from the boat and bring him to the infirmary for wound-treatment. No one was quite sure exactly what Colin's role in all this was but it sounded, for the time being, that he wasn't as guilty as we'd all thought. I sort of felt bad for thinking he was a horrible ring thief felon and super liar. Sort of. But there was still the whole painting Anna naked and calling her his stupid muse thing.

As for me? I decided to head back to Vitale's castle, where his royal highness had graciously offered E.J., Chomps, and me a room for the night.

The only thing left to do was to go back to St. Thomas, to little Eli's house, and get the DeBlume Red diamond off of his bedazzled picture frame. But that, I decided, was a job better left to the pros.

Date: Saturday
Time: 11:00 a.m.
Location: Cruz Bay Ferry almost en route to St. Thomas, eventually en route to Elkton.
Day Rating (So Far): Five glorious, sunny, 77 degree stars.

Last night, after a delicious Italian dinner of spaghetti carbonera, cheesy garlic bread, and lots and lots (and lots) of wine, Eddie, Chomps, Vitale, and I settled in for the night. Chomps had dropped Colin off at the infirmary, where he was being held overnight with a concussion and a broken heart. Eddie picked him up this morning and brought him back to Vitale's. I couldn't wait to sit him down and force him to tell me the whole story about everything. But before that, I made sure I had done all the following things:

1. Showered in Vitale's cajillion dollar granite shower complete with five showerheads and on-demand steam action. While using loads and loads of spendy fragranced shower gel.
2. Had one of Vitale's personal servants do my hair and makeup and loan me some designer threads and make me look way more awesome than I usually do.
3. Perfected my 'aloof and distant' attitude so Colin would not know if I still loved him or didn't love him at all, due to all his stupid decision making skills and missing our wedding and turn-

ing off his cell phone and making me go on my un-honeymoon alone.

Turns out, Colin really wasn't the stupid dumbass I originally thought he was. After being approached by Anna (who is, incidentally, still at large) and getting seduced by her looks and breasts and money, Colin got duped into painting some pictures under the name of 'Patrick Patrick' for the upcoming gallery auction. That way, Anna could smuggle Jimmy into the auction and the two of them could steal the ring and run away together and start a new life filled with money and rings. Colin put two and two together like the smart artist he is and went straight to the police with the whole ring stealing story.

Of course, instead of doing anything legal about it, the corrupt police officer (my sausage-armed attacker) decided to get in on the action, too. This left Colin with no one to trust and a police officer threatening to kill him and ruin his whole life if he didn't cooperate. So he did, kind of.

After Colin painted the pictures to get the fake Patrick Patrick (Jimmy) into the auction, Jimmy cornered old man Hanson in the back room while Anna busted out all the cameras and cracked the display case. Then Anna fled the gallery and ran straight into Colin. Who stole the ring from her in a fit of jealous artist rage. That double crosser! (Not really.)

Colin high tailed it back across the sea to his muse-ical mini-house, swapped out the stone, left Eli the bedazzled picture frame and his baseball cap, and flew home with the fake ring in hand. Which he then gave to me. But only because I accidentally came across it in his bureau while snooping through his things, giving him no other option but to pretend it was an engagement ring all along. Which it never was in the first place. Turns out, Colin had never even planned to propose to me. Or marry me. Dick.

Colin spent the next few months waiting out the ring stealing storm overseas, listening to me plan a wedding that never should have been planned in the first place (due to accidental engagement), *and* trying to figure out how he was going to get out of the mess he'd gotten into (due to fear of death/life ruinage). The night before our wedding, Colin got a phone call from sausage-arms. Sausage-arms had used all his police intelligence and resources to track Colin back to Minnesota and decided to threaten to kill Colin, me, and everyone else in Elkton if Colin didn't come clean with the ring. So, like an idiot, Colin flew back to the island with the idea that he would give the diamond back and save everyone he loved in the process. He figured there was no way I'd go on our honeymoon by myself. But I did. Obviously. And as soon as Colin got to the island, sausage-arms attacked him and kept him hostage like a prisoner. Then, before Colin could even wake up and explain what was going on, I showed up and started waving the ring around everywhere, throwing a wrench into all the plans.

Oops.

Luckily I solved the whole mission in the nick of time and recovered the missing diamond without anyone getting hurt at all. Except for slight head damage and moderate emotional trauma. And, because of me, Eddie got his job back with the FBI because I let him take the credit for taking down the police officer corruption. Because Eddie let me take the credit for recovering the DeBlume Red.

And the best part of all?

Vitale had promised Eddie a handsome reward for recovering the ring, which Eddie can't accept because he's a public official again and they can't ever take any dollars from anyone (right). So that means...

Drum roll please...

HE'S GIVING THE HANDSOME REWARD TO ME!

To meeeeeeeee!!!!

Meeeeeeeeee!!!

Guess what the handsome reward is? You'll never guess. Never ever, in a cajillion years.

One hundred thousand dollars!!

Hurrah!

Since I am a gentlewoman, I offered to split the handsome reward evenly between Colin, Chomps, and myself. Colin declined since he's the reason everyone got into the whole mess in the first place and Chomps couldn't accept the dollars either, also due to some public official thing. So I decided to set up a little surprise for Eli when he turns 18 since he took such good care of the $2.2M diamond picture frame while everyone was busy running around blaming each other for everything. That left $75,000 big fat green dollars with my name all over them. Minus taxes.

Seventy five thousand dollars!! Hurrah! That means I can:

1. Not have to foreclose on my over-budget townhouse.
2. Not have to call my parents for money ever again.
3. Actually go shopping with Leah and get some new digs.
4. Afford spa treatments for the rest of my life.
5. Pay off my credit card debt ($15,000).
6. Pay my dad back for my super-botched wedding.
7. Not worry if Kelly actually does fire me, because I have $75,000 (less taxes, less credit card debt, less all the other stuff I already mentioned) and have no problems telling him exactly what I think of him! Hurrah again!

As for Colin and me? Well…that's a long and difficult story. One that's become highly complicated due to my intense emotional feelings toward a certain super handsome formerly-tropical island sex god named Eddie. *Swoon.* Who lives in Washington D.C., literally half a country away from me.

Which makes going home a very difficult affair.

Yet here I am, sitting on the ferry dock with Chomps and Colin. They're both trying to read this over my shoulder, which is highly annoying and bothersome. Vitale is also here, waiting to see us off. And poor Eddie is sitting at the end of the dock looking sad and very sexy and like he hates Colin with all his might.

Confession: Eddie asked me to stay a few extra days so we could 'get to know each other' without all the lies and kidnappers standing in between us.

Confession: Colin asked me to give him a second chance now that we don't have all the lies and kidnappers standing in between us. Even though he never meant to propose to me in the first place and now I feel like the biggest losery loser in all of history.

Confession: Chomps promised my dad he'd whisk me away from all the lies and kidnappers and bring me home in one piece.

Confession: Leah never even showed up to say goodbye. In fact, no one has seen her since before the ransacking of her mansion. Jimmy swore to the police that the mansion was empty when he and Anna performed the ransacking and dumping of Colin's body in the closet, but would you trust those two? I know I wouldn't. I was really looking forward to (1) thanking Leah for actually being a good friend and bestowing free makeovers and life advice, and (2) apologizing for mistaking her for her evil twin and thinking she was a two-timing double-crossing murderess. And telling her that I now understand why she had my underpants and took all those sneaky photos of me. I would probably do that too, if I thought someone had stolen the $2.2M ring I was supposed to inherit from my highly famous and super cool grandpa.

Confession: I really don't want to go home. I hate it there. Really. It's too cold, among lots of other things.

I need a sign. Universe? Jesus? Anyone? Hello?

Date: Saturday
Time: 11:30 a.m.
Location: Cruz Bay Ferry, about to take off in mere minutes.
Day Rating (So Far): Completely life changing and super awesome in every way imaginable! A sign has arrived! Thanks guys!

There I was, sitting on the ferry, waiting for it to take off for my final journey across the sea, when the weirdest, most wonderful thing happened.

It all started with a phone call. Vitale was only on the phone for a minute when his face went pale and he started racing toward me.

"Samantha!" A voice rose over the sounds of the beach and the gently lapping beach waves.

"Huh?"

Vitale was racing toward the ferry waving both arms over his head.

"Samantha!" he cried. "Wait!"

"What the hell is that?" Colin asked over my shoulder.

"Shhhh…" I said.

"Freeze!" Chomps yelled, holding out his badge. "Elkton PD!"

"Shhhh!" I hissed. "Idiots!"

Vitale got as far as the ferry security man before he was stopped for not having a ticket. "Samantha" he called again. "I need to speak with you! Please!"

I grabbed Chomps's police badge and waved it toward the ferry security man. "Let him through," I shouted. "Police business over here!" Then a gust of wind came and I dropped the badge. It plopped into the ocean.

"My badge!" Chomps threw himself over the side of the ferry and fell into the ocean with a splash.

Colin shrugged and gazed out over the sea, showcasing his strong side profile and making me remember all the reasons I loved him (nice floppy hair, hipster coolness, etc.).

Vitale pushed past the ferry security man and strode my way.

"Stone!" he huffed, reaching the ferry at last. "That's quite the security team you have there, my dear."

I grinned.

"I'm afraid I have a problem. I need your help."

"What is it?" I asked.

"That was my pilot on the phone. He's just gotten back from McCarran and heard the news about Anna. He's sick with fright."

"Why?" I asked.

"Because she was on the plane to McCarran. With Leah."

"What?"

"Anna had my pilot fly them to McCarran last night, after Jimmy was arrested."

"Why would Leah want to go anywhere with Anna after what she did?"

Vitale looked sick. "She didn't want to," he sighed. "Anna...the pilot said Leah was half asleep the whole time. Drugged, by the looks of things."

Right. Who drugs their twin sister and kidnaps her after trying to steal her cajillion dollar inheritance? What a horrible person!

"I need you, Samantha," Vitale said. "Bring my granddaughters back home."

"But..."

I looked at Chomps, who was in the middle of wrestling his badge away from a sea creature. I looked at Colin, who was still gazing out over the ocean and tapping his fingers, certainly thinking lots of cool hipster artist thoughts and ignoring all the un-cool anti-artist dumbness around him. I looked at Eddie, still watching me from the end of the dock, leaning back against his Jeep with his tight blue jeans and his pec-hugging t-shirt and his backwards baseball cap.

"I believe the going rate is $35 an hour, plus expenses," Vitale said. "Leah and I are scheduled to be in Rome in a week for her film debut. One week, my dear. It's very important that you find her. I'll pay you double. No – *triple* – if you bring her home before we're scheduled to leave for Italy."

Wait – what? $35 an *hour*? For tracking down a couple of grown women? Triple if I do it within a week? Ohmigod, that was only like...a million times more than what I make working for Kelly. Who knew sleuthing was so awesomely lucrative anyway? On the other hand, I don't know the first thing about actually being an official sleuth. Didn't you have to get a certificate and take classes and, like, be official and everything?

Vitale read my mind. "You recovered my diamond when no one else could. I need you."

"But –" I stammered. "I'm just an HR person. All I do is update compliance handbooks and conduct sexual harassment trainings. I don't know the first thing about being a private investigator!"

"I need you, Samantha," Vitale's face clouded.

I remembered Colin lying the closet, whispering "Save Leah." Did he know something? Leah's face flashed before me. Her excitement over my free makeover. How we laughed and cried together during *Love Actually*. Now that I knew she didn't do any of those horrible things I thought she did, I felt a little indebted to her. Even if she did steal my ring. But that was only because she thought I had stolen it from her grandpa in the first place.

I sighed.

Chomps reboarded the ferry, dripping and angry. "Let's get dis show boot on da rode," he grumbled, plopping next to Colin. Colin moved over to where I had been sitting as water pooled on the seat next to Chomps.

Then my phone rang.

And it was Kelly.

Crap.

I looked at Vitale, I thought of Leah and her dumb evil sister, I thought of my parents waiting for me back home. I thought of Melody and Amanda and all my other un-friends, of my job, my townhouse. I looked at Chomps and my seat all covered with water. I looked at Colin.

I made my decision and answered my phone.

"Hello Kelly," I said.

"*Sammy!*" he roared. "I have been trying to get a hold of you all week! Did you know that we have compliance auditors here from *Minneapolis* and they are telling me that our handbooks are out of date? Out of date! What do I pay you for anyway? And why the *hell* haven't you called me back? When I call you, I expect an answer. My expectation is –"

"Hey Kelly?" I tried to interrupt his rambling. He kept rambling.

"Hey Kelly?" I interrupted again. "Kelly? Hello? I'm talking here."

"How *dare* you speak to me like that. I am your superior. I am a Vice President. I am —"

"— a huge fucking asshole," I finished for him. "I know. Everyone knows. Oh, by the way? Don't ever call me again. I quit."

Then I hung up, turned off my phone, and turned to Vitale.

"Where did you say the plane dropped them off?" I asked him.

Vitale grinned. "McCarran."

Right. "And where is that...exactly?"

Vitale's face fell. "Oh dear," he said. He looked at Eddie, standing alone at the end of the dock. "You may want to bring some help. McCarran International Airport, my dear. Las Vegas."

"Las Vegas?" I said. "As in..."

As in Viva Las Vegas? Hotels? Glitter? Glamour? Legal prostitution? All-night casinos? The Rat Pack? Free beverages? No clocks? Hmmm...I could do classes, I thought to myself. I could get a certificate. I could get official. I could definitely go to Las Vegas.

I shook my bangs and grinned at Vitale. "When do I start?"

(Note to future self: research how to be a better sleuth; become a better sleuth.)

###

Acknowledgments

Thanks to everyone I know.
(And, in case I missed anyone, thanks to all the
other people, too. Plus cats, dogs, unicorns,
et cetera. I could not have done this without you.)

Don't miss the next Samantha Stone adventure,
What Happened in Vegas.
Available July 2015.

Made in the USA
Lexington, KY
22 December 2015